Hell Awaits

Erin Louis

Printed in the United States of America

Dedication

Dedicated to my own pot-smoking, sewing demon.

1

"There's nothing quite like the smell of blood after an orgy," Satan said to Kat. Her name was Kathryn, but he never called her Kathy. Satan was cool like that. He handed her a faux goat horn pipe full of the dankest green bud in Hell. Satan always had the best weed. It's a faux goat horn because any kind of cruelty to animals in Hell will get you a fast-track ticket for a dip in the lake of fire. Kat had seen it happen, and it's not pretty. The skin grows back relatively quickly, but it's still not any kind of cute. It's better just not to be a dick to any animals in Hell. And for the most part, no one is. In fact, people aren't usually dicks to each other either. Hell is cool like that, too.

She took a long hit off the pipe, and passed it to her left, where the next naked person in the Satanic cuddle puddle took it with a smile. They were all lying on a giant soft shag rug in the middle of Satan's orgy room. Kat couldn't be sure but guessed there were somewhere around forty people in all. All hand selected by Satan of course. And all from his waiting list, which is somewhere between an eternity and infinity long. Satan is the fairest person, or deity she had ever met. Granted, Kat had only ever met two deities. His ethics are impeccable really, especially in comparison to the other guy. She found out the hard way that God is a dick. And Satan's orgies are no satanic ethical exception. They are the hottest thing in Hell. Figuratively speaking of course, the lake of fire is literally the hottest thing in Hell. Held once a week, he carefully curated the invites in the order of the list. Making sure everyone had their chance in due time. Also making sure that the group has aligning tastes. An epic orgy wouldn't be quite so epic if half of them have a foot fetish, and the other half is hopelessly ticklish. Everyone who wants to got their turn, in time. This being the afterlife, there is plenty of that. The good news was that aging wasn't really a thing in Hell. Everybody that came to Hell showed up around their prime age, or at least Kat thought so. Twenties or thirties or so. Similar to Heaven, but not in the perfected bodies of angels. Every scar, blemish, and split end came to Hell with you while Heaven erased them.

It was warm and a bit musky in the room, but the windows were open, and a light breeze brought a subtle coolness to the atmosphere. Although the orgy had ended, everyone having gotten theirs, a few people were still moaning and breathing heavily. Orgasms in Hell are really something. In fact, they are rumored to be very literally earth moving. Kat wondered if she were to check the news reports on earth, if she would see an earthquake somewhere about once a week that would just so happen to correspond to one of Satan's legendary orgies.

She lifted her head to the scent on the wind as it ruffled her dark brown hair and cooled the sweat on her brow. It smelled of iron. Outside a rainstorm had just passed over, the ground would be soaked in blood. But it would be fully absorbed by the time she is ready to leave. While she didn't find the smell after it rains in Hell quite as pleasant as the smell of rain on earth, she had grown fond of it. It was no fun to get caught in a rainstorm in Hell, if only because blood stains are a bitch to get out no matter what realm you resided in, but the plants were nothing short of amazing. Her own little yard was now as lush and full of flowers as it had been in Heaven. Of course, in Hell, she had to tend to them herself. But boy, did blood ever make great fertilizer.

The pipe came around again but was empty when it got back to the big guy. He dipped into his stash to refill it before handing it to Kat again. He smiled at her as she took a long drag. Kat smiled back at him, partly because she had grown to like him a lot. But mostly because the horns on his head had been temporarily replaced by penises, and he had yet to change them back. They were no longer erect, and so they hung limp on the sides of his huge red face. She suspected he knew that he looked silly and was simply choosing to sport his limp head dicks for the sake of her and the other participant's amusement. Satan was a bit of a card.

This wasn't Kat's first orgy in Hell, but it was her first with Satan himself, and probably the last one with him for a long time. As she would go back down to the bottom of the wait list. And she had to admit, it kind of took the cake. Her legs might as well have been made of Jello as she tried to stand up. It could have been the weed she supposed, but more likely the multiple orgasms. She had been in Hell for a while now, and while Amon the demon was still her main squeeze, they both enjoyed the company of others on occasion.

As the exhausted but supremely satisfied guests started to stir, said their goodbyes and headed for the exit, Satan gently took her wrist and said, "Kat, would you stick around for a few? I'd like to talk to you."

Kat sat back down, not because there would be any repercussions if she didn't, but because she respected the guy. Satan saw his guests to the door hugging them and planting kisses on their cheeks and foreheads. When they were alone, he came back to the rug, gathered some pillows and sat next to her. Kat reached up and poked one of the limp appendages which now hung in front of one eye, giving him a phallic emo vibe. He jiggled them back and forth with an ugly but endearing smile.

"Have you given any thought to my offer," he said to her.

Kat looked down at her lap. She had. But was still unsure of her answer. She had run into Satan a few times since escaping the nightmare that was Heaven. And each time she expected him to ask her this very question. But he hadn't until now. True to his word, he wanted her to get acclimated to her new environment. Although, as she looked at him now, she wondered if he had been waiting for this very moment. For her turn to come up for the orgy when she was dripping with the afterglow… among other things. But she dismissed the thought as soon as it came. Satan just wasn't manipulative like that. He was sincere and pure in his intentions. She had learned through her own experience with him, but also by talking with the other inhabitants of Hell.

"I have. But I guess I'm still not sure about it," she said, lifting her head to look at him. "I have…questions, but mostly I'm afraid."

"Well, let's start with your questions and maybe that will help alleviate your fears."

Kat thought for a moment, "Ok, so what exactly would I be doing? And for fuck's sake, how? And why me?"

"Here, take another hit," he handed her the pipe, which was comically small in his big hands. She was momentarily distracted by her recent memory of his huge fingers, but then he began to speak again. "First, you know better than anyone else how deceptive Heaven is. How unjust, and how unfair it is. There's no one here in Hell other than myself who has seen it for themselves. As hard as I try to make things easy and frankly… fun," he jiggled his flaccid head dicks again, "telling people that God is a dick and that Heaven sucks, just isn't an easy sell. Even people that know and trust me think I'm full of shit. It's fucking Heaven after all. Or not fucking

Heaven," and with that, he let out a horrific but yet somehow sweet snort laugh.

"You definitely have the market cornered on fucking in the afterlife," she said, and was surprised to hear her own snort laugh.

"So that's the 'why you part'. There really is no one else I could ask. I mean you've spoken to God. Not to mention talked shit to Saint Peter. You really are my hero Kat. I mean that."

Kat blushed and took a minute to ponder the fact that she was Satan's hero, her mother would be horrified, if not totally surprised.

"Well, thank you. I can't say I feel like much of hero, and it wasn't intentional. So, I guess that's why I'm skeptical that I'm the right person for this."

"It *has* to be you Kat. You understand the suffering that happens at the hand of God like no one else. Most people are too terrified of me and Hell, having been taught that their whole lives. There are people that need you. As for your question about exactly what you'd be doing, you would be saving people like yourself. You reached people there and exposed the lie, and now those souls are stuck there, miserable as you were. As for the how, well…I figured we'd work that out together."

"What if I got stuck there? What if I get caught and they won't let me leave?"

Kat's guts, or whatever she had in place of guts, churned. The thought of going back to Heaven and getting trapped there again, probably a prisoner in her own perfect little house, Stryper forever blasting from her perfect speakers, or maybe worse, Creed. The image of a redeemed Jeffrey Dahmer sneering from his house next door forever nauseated her to her very core. Here she was staring in the face of Satan, the scent of blood in the air, and absolutely mortified at the thought of going back to Heaven. The donuts in heaven had been pretty great though. They tended to be always just on the edge of stale in Hell.

Satan was looking at her through eyes that should have, and maybe at one point would have, simply made her piss herself. But they didn't. In those black eyes, she saw love of all things. Love, empathy and concern for the souls he knew to be suffering. Emotions she hadn't seen in God's eyes. God's eyes held nothing but a selfish need for adoration and servitude. She had seen exactly nothing in Jesus' eyes, although she hadn't bothered to look all that closely. And the angels, what a nightmare they were. Far worse than any of the vapid, self-absorbed strippers she had worked with on earth.

Satan took her hand in his enormous and surprisingly supple one, her thoughts turned again to his lengthy, strong, and talented fingers, and said, "Kat, I will not ever let that happen."

Kat laid back on the plush pillows and closed her eyes. Her memories didn't fade as they had in Heaven. All the horror came back to her. Like a movie she hadn't wanted to see, images of sneering angels, redeemed serial killers, and all of the mindless drones who thought they were reaping the rewards of a life worshipping a sadistic narcissist who had them convinced He loved them. That their suffering on earth and devotion to Him, was all for their own benefit. The whole thing was so twisted.

And then there was her father.

Alone in his perfect heaven house, with his dog, and his endless bottle of scotch. Kat's heart flipped. Could she just leave him there? He wasn't happy, but he was content. Sort of. He was drunk, not content, she had to admit to herself. Hell was…well Hell. But it was honest. It was transparent. It didn't hold the lie of Heaven. She hadn't been able to convince him of that, or her Aunt Judy, but now that she had escaped would they listen to her? Was it her place to even try?

Kat's head began to ache a little at the sour memories of Heaven. On earth she had been a less than ethical stripper. An unbeliever, she didn't think there was any kind of an afterlife. And she definitely hadn't thought she would get into Heaven if there was one. Her harrowing and enlightening trip to Heaven had left her a better person, albeit still a dead one. And she was happy in Hell.

She owed most of it to Amon though. Without him, she would still be miserable in Heaven. Never knowing the truth about Hell. And while they weren't exclusive, their love was pure. Did she want to risk losing the one guy she had actually fallen in love with to rescue people in Heaven? Satan promised her that he wouldn't let her be trapped there, but how much power did he really have against God?

"Can I think on it a little more?" Kat asked Satan, his horns had returned their normal menacing and less hilarious state. His expression had turned serious also.

"Of course, my love. I know you're scared. And you're probably right to be. I haven't tested my powers against God in ages." Kat was only slightly alarmed at the fact that he seemed to have plucked that thought out of her head. But alarm as an emotion in Hell was really pretty relative. "But please give it some serious consideration. We could make a formidable team. And do some good for people in the process." He smiled a smile that had she not known him, would have made her faint. Instead, it made her smile back. "Can I give you a lift home?"

"You can," Kat said with a smile. And Satan lifted her in his arms and carried her all the way back to her little home in Hell.

2

Satan kissed Kat goodbye and smiled at her, saying nothing as he turned on his hoofs to walk back to wherever he was going to next. Lucifer was waiting just inside her front door as she walked in.

"Kat! You're naked!" Lucifer said, putting one paw over his eye as if he were embarrassed. He wasn't.

"I'm also filthy," she replied with a wink.

She picked up the furry little beast and kissed his head. She hadn't liked the little bastard when God gave him to her in Heaven. He was supposed to replace Buster, her cat who had died with her in the car crash and had been sent straight to Hell. Although he had technically caused the crash, she didn't think he belonged in Hell. No one in Heaven wanted to tell her that he had been sent to Hell of course, so she worried about him the whole damned time, not knowing that Buster had actually been the lucky one.

She resented Lucifer's very existence, as she resented God's attempt to replace her real cat. She had named him out of spite. But he had grown on her, and she had been able to grant him the gift of speech which turned out to be a very good thing. She had also granted him a butthole, which didn't turn out to be such a good thing. No matter where they were, cats were prone to showing off their buttholes. Lucifer was no exception.

Buster sat on the couch, doing his best to appear still mad at her. But she knew he wasn't really. His thin veneer of hate for her crumbled as soon as she put Lucifer down and walked over to him. She scratched the spot between his ears, and he began to purr in spite of himself. She bent down to plant a kiss on his head. Buster never could talk and didn't in Hell. When Lucifer came to Hell, she had thought that he had lost his voice, but it turned out that he was just terrified. It didn't take long for him to find it again. And he made use of it every chance he got.

Kat went to her kitchen to check the cat food dishes. They were mostly full, but she filled them to the top anyway. Of all the weird things in Hell, the abject mediocrity of most things, the cat food was high end. She filled their water bowl also before heading to the bathroom to check the litter box.

There had been no poop in Heaven, mostly because there were no buttholes. Although, she had found a loophole for that problem. That was not the case in Hell. The litter box was nothing short of a horror show. Rather than scoop the lumps, she took the whole thing outside and dumped it, rinsed it out with a hose, and brought it back inside to fill with fresh litter. She performed this task still naked, because in Hell, naked was perfectly fine should one choose to be. And the climate was always warm and cozy.

Her hell cats snuggled each other on the couch, Buster having dropped his own resentment of Lucifer. Kat suspected that if Buster had been able to talk, he wouldn't admit that fact. And after Lucifer dropped his fear of Buster, the two had become good friends. Or at least snuggle buddies. She smiled at them and went back into the bathroom to rinse the orgy off herself. She washed her hair, and soaped up once, and then again just for good measure. All the time pondering Satan's job offer.

She knew she probably should do it. She would have Hell on her side. But aside from the fear she felt about going back, and possibly not being able to return to Hell, she wondered if it was the right thing to do. The people in Heaven spent their entire lives hoping to get there. Would she be the asshole if she tried to change their minds? God and Jesus's entire shtick was to change the minds of people and convince them to love a monster, all the while telling them it was humans who were the monsters. And in most cases, they had succeeded.

Aunt Judy was a prime example, she loved her hoard of cats. She lost her weed connection when the portal where Amon had come through and helped Kat and Lucifer out of Hell. But like her brother, she had found peace at the bottom of a heavenly bottle. And she certainly wasn't lonely after Kat had shown her how to make her cats talk, and how to give them treats and food. The consequence of which was that they acquired buttholes. Did Kat want to take that away from her in favor of a truth she may not even want?

The water had run cold, it hadn't actually been that hot to begin with, just warm, and Kat turned it off. She got out and toweled off with a towel that could have been softer but was clean and smelled nice. As fun as the orgy had been, she was happy to be clean and to smell like soap and not bodily fluids. Her bathroom was pleasantly warm as she wrapped her hair in another towel and rubbed her body with lotion. She looked at herself in the mirror before dabbing a bit of zit cream on the pimple she saw forming there. In Heaven she had been blemish free, not so much in Hell. But Heaven had made her appreciate her zits of all things. She smirked at the thought. Her new eternal home was full of enlightenment.

Her small bedroom held a small dresser from which she plucked a dark green soft velour zip up onesie. She stepped into it and inhaled the scent of clean laundry. There was no laundry to do in Heaven. And so, there was no clean laundry smell. It was mid-morning already, on a Sunday. She probably had some chores to do, but she was tired after the all-night shenanigans, so she decided she would treat herself to a long day on the couch with her cats. She nuked a frozen burrito and carried it, along with a large glass of water and slightly brown spotted banana, to her living room.

She clicked on the TV and turned it to a rerun of the Twilight Zone. It was all reruns in Hell because it was Hell she supposed. But it was her favorite episode at least. The one where the poor guy, who just wanted time to read, finds himself in a post-apocalyptic world where he had all the time and all the books. He's in his own personal Heaven, until he breaks his glasses.

She finished eating and lit up her pipe, choosing to put Satan's request off her mind. A long break from thinking about it should bring some clarity. She thought that later she would speak to Amon about it. They had already talked ad nauseum on the subject, but he was patient with her. Listening without judgment or trying to sway her one way or the other. He was not a fan of the idea, as he was as afraid to lose her, as she was him. God, she loved him. It was with thoughts of her demon lover in Hell that Kat drifted off to sleep.

A soft knock at the door woke her up sometime later. She had been dreaming of being on stage again, it had turned into a bit of a nightmare. In her dream, she had a knot in her bikini top and was struggling to get it undone as her audience grew restless. Sneers and giggles began to spread throughout the crowd, and she was grateful to be woken. The knock came again, and she got up, fully expecting it to be Amon. But when she opened the door, she found Lyla instead.

Since Kat dragged the horrible mean girl angel to Hell, Lyla had undergone a remarkable transformation. In Heaven, Lyla had been one of God's favorite angels. Beautiful to the point of almost being painful to look at. She had been one of the worst bullies Kat had ever encountered, both in life and the after part. But in Hell, she was as she had been on earth.

Overweight with bad skin and hair, she nearly fainted when she climbed the stone steps to the entrance to Hell. She cried non-stop at first, wanting nothing more than to get back to Heaven. Kat's pity had only gone so far, considering the suffering she had caused.

But Lyla had not just grown accustomed to Hell, she embraced it. Perhaps finally remembering how others had treated her in her own life, Lyla was now kind and thoughtful. She was curvy and had worked hard to get strong. She cut and styled her hair and took care of her skin. As she stood in front of Kat now, she looked happy and healthy, with no trace of the cruelty she wore in Heaven. Kat found her to be far more beautiful now than she had been in Heaven. Lyla had found love too. Or lust, she embraced her inner slut and was very popular. She had been popular in Heaven, but for all the wrong reasons. In Hell, her popularity came from her newfound confidence in her body and her compassion for other souls. That confidence and compassion made her sexy as…well Hell. Hell had been very good for this angel.

Kat was only slightly disappointed to see that it was Lyla and not Amon, "Hey Lyla! Come in." She stepped aside to let the fallen angel into her home. Lucifer looked up and gave her a bit of a dirty look. He stood up, turned around and lifted his tail, making sure she had a good long look at his butthole, before going back to sleep. He hadn't quite forgiven her for her transgressions in Heaven. He may have been a Heaven cat, but he could hold a grudge like an earth cat.

"Hi Kat!" Lyla beamed and locked her into a bear hug, before accepting the invitation to come inside.

They sat on the couch, and Kat picked up her banana peel and burrito plate from the chipped coffee table.

"Can I get you something to drink?"

"Sure, how about some wine?" Lyla asked hopefully.

"I think I got some hooch in the kitchen. I'll be right back."

Kat poured herself another glass of water and filled a tumbler halfway with the boxed wine she had in her fridge. She found she didn't drink much in Hell. But she kept some wine for company, mostly Lyla. Of all the unexpected things, that she would become friends with Lyla was the most surprising.

"Thank you," Lyla said as she sipped her almost good wine.

"What's up?"

"Well…." Lyla beamed, and put her left hand in the air, where a very obvious fake diamond sat in a yellow gold band on her ring finger. "I'm getting married!"

"Congrats! But the boys are going to be disappointed. The girls too." Kat smiled back at her. Among other things, Lyla had discovered she wasn't strictly dickly.

"Oh no. We have an open relationship."

"I'm so happy for you. You deserve all the good things," Kat said and meant every word. Lyla had been a twat-waffle of the highest order, but the work she had done and all the help she had done for others, she really did deserve all the good things.

"What's going on with you?" Lyla asked, draining her glass.

"Well, for one, Satan wants me to go back to Heaven to rescue the souls who don't want to be there."

"Ooo…that sounds fun," Lyla said, but then frowned. "Or maybe not. I can't believe I'm going to say this but that place sucks."

"Yeah, and I guess that's the whole point. I've found some peace here, and I can't stand the thought of going back and not being able to come home."

Lyla took a long sip of her wine, "I get that. But what you did getting out of there, was nothing short of a miracle." She smirked at that, "You showed people the truth of that place. At least the ones who were willing to listen."

"And now those people are there miserable, knowing the truth. I'm not sure I did them any favors. I guess this would be my chance to right that wrong." Kat sipped her water and picked back up her pipe again.

"The worst humans on earth, the ones who found redemption in God, but without actually being good people are the ones who are really enjoying it up there."

Kat thought of her Heavenly but utterly vile neighbors, "I wonder if Satan would let me bring them here? Like I could rescue the good people but also get a few of the assholes down here where they could see just a little bit of justice." Kat thought of the Hitler rally she had come upon in Heaven. He was the epitome of redemption in God's eyes, proof that anyone could be saved from Hell.

"Huh…," Lyla pondered. "Sounds like a holy pissing contest. You'd be taking on God himself. That's pretty ballsy my friend."

"Or profoundly stupid. They would recognize me in a second," Kat said.

"They totally would. It's a terrible idea, Kat," Lucifer said. Kat had thought he had been sleeping, but apparently not. "They'd trap you and keep you. And you'd be miserable, plus…"

Kat put her hand on his head between his ears, and he couldn't talk around his purr. Buster was awake and wore a look of profound disapproval. Buster always wore that look, on earth and in Hell, but Kat knew this time he was disapproving of her going on this mission.

"I know little dude," Kat said, using her other hand to scratch under Buster's chin. She had loved cats mostly because of their low maintenance in comparison to dogs, but she was rethinking that logic now.

"Well, if it were me, I think I'd say no," Lyla said. "It's much too dangerous. And like you said, they'd recognize you in a second."

Kat picked up her pipe from the coffee table and held it up for Lyla, who shook her head no. Kat took a long hit and closed her eyes. Her whole life she had been taught to resist Satan. That he and his dark forces would lead her in the wrong direction. The irony was not lost on her that now that she was in Hell, and Satan her friend, she was thinking about refusing him.

Kat had learned that Satan wasn't the bad guy, not by a long shot. Just another lie meant to scare her into submission. And it was with that thought that she made up her mind. Enough with the lies. Enough with the deception, she had succeeded once, and she would do it again.

"You know…Fuck it. I don't know how yet, but I'm going to do it."

3

As she walked to Satan's place, Kat was having second thoughts. Or maybe third and fourth thoughts. Lucifer had kind of freaked out after Lyla left. Buster seemed perturbed, but she couldn't be totally sure if that was because she had decided to go on Satan's mission, or if he was simply perturbed. Lucifer was so upset that he didn't even try to talk her out of it. He didn't talk at all. Just looked at her with his sad big eyes that made her feel like the biggest asshole in Hell. She knew she wasn't quite the biggest asshole, that was probably reserved for some real sociopaths, but she felt like an asshole just the same. Lucifer slunk into her bedroom, staring at her with those glassy eyes that reflected her utter betrayal. Cats were so dramatic. They both slept on the sofa when she had gone to bed, and Lucifer still wouldn't talk to her when she woke.

But she could see why he felt that way. She was the reason he existed, if you took God out of the equation. He was created for her, and if she were to not make it back, he would be here without her. Buster on the other hand, was here because she couldn't find the stupid pet carrier. Had she found it, or canceled his appointment none of them would be here together at all. He might have the best reason of all for being pissed. Even if pissed was Buster's default mode. When she was alive, she knew that she had disappointed the people in her life. Mostly her mother, and in death she had hoped that she was making up for that. She wanted to make things right, but not at the further expense of those that cared about her.

The storm that had passed the day before had left the ground slightly mushy as she walked. Her sneakers left soft impressions in the darkened dirt. There weren't any clouds in the sky and Kat marveled at the winged demons doing loop-de-loops over her head. Hell had many kinds of demons. Some were like Amon, he looked like a person but had never been alive on earth. And some were sort of animal-like creatures, goblins of sorts she thought. Not human like at all, but part of this otherworldly eco system. And then there were the cats. While all dogs ended up in Heaven, Hell was the domain of cats in the afterlife. They were everywhere. Not all of them had homes, but they all had shelter and food. She remembered how pissed she had been when she had been told that Buster had gone to Hell. But it was a needless worry because no cat went uncared for in Hell. Hell of all places seemed to be cat paradise. Some dogs made it to Hell, but they tended to be pretty scarce.

She passed Amon's house, and almost stopped, but instead kept walking. Maybe she would end up backing out of this screwball idea, but at the very least she thought she should talk to Satan first. Get some more details about how it might all work. Kat couldn't pretend that the idea of fucking with God and righting some of his fucked-up wrongs didn't excite her a little. In fact, it excited her a lot. It felt good to feel like she had a purpose. Other than caring for her cats eternally.

Four demons were playing volleyball just outside of the gated entrance to Satan's giant stone mansion. They weren't human type demons, but kind you might see in a horror movie, red skin with horns on their heads. Genderless, they were Satan's minions. Not slaves but well-loved servants. Created to do Satan's bidding, and it wasn't hard to see that they enjoyed their jobs. It was also easy to see that they were quite good at volleyball. She had been watching their game as she approached the large gates. Not once had the volleyball touched the ground, but as she approached one of them set the ball and the other spiked it hard on the other side of the net.

"Owww!" The ball cried as it smashed into the ground, and Kat cringed when she realized it wasn't quite a ball. She had noticed that it wasn't white, or symmetrical as a normal volleyball would be as she had walked toward the game. But now she saw that it was a human head. At least she assumed it was human or had been at some point. A headless body sat to the side in a military uniform, which had she paid more attention in history class she would have recognized as Stalin's.

The demons laughed as they picked up the whining head, moved away from the net and proceeded to begin a game of soccer. The head moaned and cried. Each time a cloven hoof struck, the head cried out louder and Kat cringed again. The demons paused briefly to curtsy to Kat as she stepped through the open iron gates, she nodded back. The polite demons went back to their game as she started up the steps to the front door. As she put her hand on the giant metal ball sack door knocker, she heard a splat, a yelp, then more demon laughter. She cringed again and knocked on the door.

Another of Satan's minions answered her knock with a curtsy and a smile. "He's been expecting you, right this way."

Satan's foyer was nothing short of spectacular. Done in what Kat thought, but probably wouldn't have articulated out loud, was a predictable red velvet and black décor. Black and purple roses sat on a huge round table. Two winding staircases bracketed each side of the room, with a dark hallway that ran down the middle of the space. Kat had been here several times before, but each time she noticed a detail that she had missed on the previous visits. This time it was the candelabras on the walls. There were no electric lights, only long red candles that sat in black metal holders. The tiny flickering flames cast shadows on the wall as the demon led her up the dark red carpeted staircase to the left.

On the wall at the top of the landing was a huge portrait of Lemmy Kilmister in a pair of way too short cutoff jeans. Kat thought if she cared to look more closely, she might see a clandestine bit of ball sack. A cigarette hung out of the side of his mouth, and his eyes stared right through Kat as she passed the framed painting. The demon led her down the hallway to the end, where they curtsied again and turned to leave. Kat raised her hand to knock on the black wooden door, but it swung open before she had a chance.

"Come," Satan boomed. "Then come again if you like," and he snort laughed.

"Hello," Kat said, trying and failing to match his enthusiasm.

He was lying in the middle of his huge red round bed on top of a red velvet bedspread. Kat was surprised to see he wasn't naked but instead wore a purple jogging suit. It stretched across his broad chest, almost straining to contain his bulk. Kat thought that Satan could really use a tailor, and an interior decorator if she were being honest. The poor guy was a walking cliché.

"I'm so glad you're here. Are you hungry? Can I get you something to drink?"

"No thanks, I'm good," she replied.

"Oh, I so hope my friends and their game out front didn't ruin your appetite. I should really have them set up behind the house." He patted a space next to him on the bed and Kat began to climb up to sit next to him.

"I have to admit, it was a little off putting. I thought by now I would be more used to that kind of thing."

"My bad, but trust me, that guy earned every bit of that and more."

Kat believed him.

"I guess you know why I'm here," she said.

"I do. I hope with good news…" Satan replied.

"Well, I think so."

"Splendid!" Satan grabbed her up in a bear hug so tight she thought her ribs were going to crack. She had intended to tell him maybe, and that she wanted a few more details before committing. But now as she was enveloped in his arms, she felt like that opportunity had passed. This was going to happen.

When he finally let her go, and she could breathe she said, "Ok, well what's the plan?"

Satan's black eyes lit up, "So I was thinking another portal would be the way to go. Sneak you in as Amon did. Of course, it would have to be in a different spot this time."

"You think they would allow another portal? Don't you think they would notice this time?"

"Oh, no. The best thing about a narcissist is that they don't tend to think they can be fooled once, and especially not twice. Plus, I don't think anyone would expect me to try the same thing again."

"Again? It was you that set up the portal where I met Amon?" Kat had never given much thought to how the portal had been set up the first time. She had just been so excited to find the demon that had been her aunt's weed plug.

"Oh yes. I set that up to screw with heaven and their no weed policy. Cause fuck all that. I fuck with God every chance I get. He does the same to me. Look at Scientology? It wasn't me that inspired L Ron Hubbard to start that crazy cult bullshit, that was all Him. Now every time one of those whack-a-doodles dies, they end up here all pissed off they're not on their alien planet. Kirsty Alley still thinks there's a spaceship coming to get her. She keeps screaming, 'but I'm clear!'"

"Oh wow. I always liked Shelley Long better anyway," Kat mused. "Ugh, that means you're going to get stuck with Tom Cruise."

"Right? I told you God is a real motherfucker. Now Joeseph Smith and the Mormon crap? All me," Satan's laugh hit her deep in the bowels. "Those fuckers are technically Christian, so to Heaven they go."

"They must be in a different part of Heaven than where I was. Way too much booze up there I would think."

"Yeah, God makes different Heavens for different believers. He doesn't much care about what flavor the belief is, as long as they believe in Him. The fighting it causes feeds His ego I assume." Kat had read somewhere about there being something like forty thousand different flavors of Christianity.

Kat nodded her head in agreement. Satan's assessment certainly fit with her experience. Meeting God had chilled her to her core. Satan had been scary sure, but that fear dissolved quickly once she got to know him. Really, as soon as she had shaken his hand. Despite his horrific appearance, Satan just had a really mellow vibe. God not so much. She didn't think it was just the weed either.

"Ok, so you open another portal, then what?" Kat asked. Satan had packed a pipe, this one in the shape of a large dick. He pursed his lips around the tip and took a hit, then passed it to her.

"Then you find the souls who want to come here and bring them back. Easy peasy, lemon squeezy," he croaked as he blew out an enormous cloud of smoke. Kat didn't think he had really thought this out.

"So, I like what, go door to door. Hand out pamphlets perhaps?"

"No, that would be annoying as fuck. But yeah, you'll have to make contact somehow. Maybe door to door but with joints?" Kat knew there would be logistics to figure out, but she had expected Satan to do the heavy lifting. She closed her eyes and thought about it as she took another hit off the dick pipe.

"Well, first off, they are going to recognize me. So, what can we do to change my looks?"

"I can't change your facial structure, so we dye and cut your hair. I'm sure I can find a makeup artist who can do some tricks too. Like I said, the great thing about someone with an ego like God's, is that they really don't ever expect to be conned. He knows He can't be fooled, that He's wrong about, that is irrelevant. The important thing is that He believes He can't be fooled," Satan smirked.

"Ahh… I see what you did there," Kat winked.

"He's probably already figured out how to pin your escape on someone else. Or maybe just covered up the whole thing. You just come in like a devout fresh soul and start sneaking people out. Avoid the ass kissing angels and you're golden."

"Hiding in plain sight can be pretty effective, especially when dealing with someone that thinks they can't be wrong." She thought of all the customers, wallets she had pilfered as a stripper. They were looking right at her as she ripped them off. She had to admit, this job was kind of made for her. "And if I get caught?"

"I've thought a lot about that," Kat was relieved he had given *some* thought to this whole thing. "And I don't think God wants that kind of fight. It would really make Him look bad. I bet He would just send you back here. Probably make a show of it too to show how awful…" he rolled his eyes, "…Hell is. And if not, I'll lead an army from Hell myself to come get you. A war ensemble if you will. He really wouldn't want that, even if He thought He could win. Imagine how weak He would look."

Satan had a point. Kat was no psychologist, but she had a club manager once who, while lacking the power of deity, had an ego just about the size of God's, and nothing scared that fucker like appearing weak to those who bought into his façade.

"Well, ok then. When do we do this?"

"How about now?" Satan said. He clapped his hands and several of his minions came bounding into the room. "We need a makeover for this little lady stat, and if you could fetch Albert, please."

4

Kat was not surprised to see the demon hairdressers and make-up artists come into the room with a chair and their corresponding equipment and supplies almost immediately. She was a bit leery about letting demons give her a haircut. On earth, Kat had been really particular about who she let touch her hair. But she was dead. And this was Hell. Kat had all of eternity to grow it back.

They set it all up in the middle of the room. Complete with rinsing bowl and portable sink. It was all quite impressive. The two demons looked excited to get started. She sat in the chair and let them drape her with the drop cloth. Satan watched from the bed, taking tokes from his pipe. The demons were ready to go to work but lacked direction.

"Bobby," Satan said to one of the demons, "Kat here needs an entirely new look. Most importantly she needs to be unrecognizable." Bobby nodded their head and chewed a claw while appearing to ponder Kat's new look, then lifted their claw to her face. Just before Bobby raked a sharp claw down her cheeks, Satan said, "Nooo! Not like that!" Bobby looked disappointed but nodded in understanding. Kat shivered at the thought of how close she had come to a new face and not just a new haircut. Satan addressed the other demon, "Sam, go get us some snacks please."

Kat had no idea how Satan could tell the two demons apart, or all of his demon servants in fact. They had no differing characteristics whatsoever. Kat simply assumed that it must be a deity thing. Or maybe like when you are friends with twins, there comes a point where no matter how much they look the same, you learn to tell them apart. Either way, Bobby took a long time sizing her up but then appeared to make a decision. They began to pour different foul-smelling substances into a small mixing bowl. Bobby was humming a tune she couldn't quite put her finger on as they worked.

Sam came back just as Bobby was starting to slather the concoction on Kat's head. Sam was pushing a small silver catering cart piled high with all sorts of delicacies. Its assortment of fruit, cheeses, and meats made her mouth water. She noticed there were no vegetables though as she picked up a plate off the cart and filled it as Bobby worked.

"No veggies?" Kat asked Satan as she took a bite of an apple slice.

"Nope, I hate them. Pretty sure God invented brussels sprouts and are literally a cruel joke on his creations."

Kat laughed and marveled at how, although she assumed it came from Satan's private food stash, her apple was still slightly mealy. She didn't want to say it out loud, lest it hurt his feelings, but she was looking forward to eating in Heaven. Even if only temporarily. She longed for some of that odd orange colored fruit that grew on the trees there. Fruit that seemed exclusive to Heaven and for which she had given to Amon in exchange for his pot.

There was no need to trade anything for weed in Hell, Satan had made it available to any who wanted to partake. Most other things had a cost, not money, but work or trade of some sort. Money wasn't much of a thing in Hell. In fact, it wasn't a thing at all. The souls in Hell could get what they wanted with some effort. Unlike in Heaven, where every desire was only a wish a way. Getting everything you wanted, with the noted exception of not being able to leave, felt really empty.

As Kat laid her head back to be rinsed, Satan addressed someone who had come into the room. But in German. Kat didn't understand a word. And with her hair under water and her head in the hands of a demon, she couldn't look up to see who it was. The conversation was brief, and from what she could tell, cordial.

She heard soft footsteps leave the room just as she was lifted up and her head wrapped up in a towel. Softer than her own at least. Bobby briskly rubbed her hair in the towel like a poodle at the groomer and began to hum again. But this time she recognized it. Then felt kind of dumb she had missed it. Motorhead, I'm so Bad (Baby I don't care). Bobby had taste it would seem.

"The portal should be ready to go in the morning," Satan said. "Thank God, we got most of the physicists." He laughed, and Kat realized something she had missed.

"Was that Albert Einstein?"

"Of course! God really screwed up there. The price he pays for demanding worship," He laughed again. "The physics of the afterlife aren't what they are on earth, but it's a good start. One of the reasons I'm not that worried if they try to keep you Kat. Hell is full of people who enjoy solving a problem. Hell's army will be made up of scientists. And big scary demons. We'll have plenty of those too."

"I guess that makes me feel better." And it did. For the most part.

Kat was more worried at the moment about the big scary scissors this Motorhead humming demon was wielding. She was at least comforted by the fact that they didn't seem interested in rearranging her face anymore. Just her hair. And now she saw large clumps of hair falling down. She struggled to see what color it was. She knew she wasn't a brunette anymore. But the hair that fell around her was wet and dark, and so colorless to her. Bobby stopped cutting and began to dry and style her hair.

"Ok, so probably a dumb question," she asked a smiling Satan. "But how come you can't just change people's looks? Like your uh… horns. Or how you can in Heaven?"

"No worries. There are no stupid questions, just profoundly stupid people. In Hell, I don't want to control the souls that come here. I can dispense justice, but beyond that, individual autonomy is the foundation of Hell. Changing your hair or make up and whatever in Heaven is only part of the illusion. It's a parlor trick meant to keep up the façade of choice."

When Satan waxed philosophical, he obtained a very serious and somber expression. It was one that Kat didn't really enjoy. While she trusted him, liked him, his appearance was still disturbing even on his best days. Kat loved that he was so willing to answer her questions honestly and directly. But she preferred the humorous Satan with the flaccid penises hanging from his head.

"I suppose that makes sense. You really think they aren't going to know who I am?"

Bobby stood in front of her having finished his work and looked to Satan for approval. Satan nodded.

"It's… certainly… different," Satan winced and then began to laugh.

Kat's stomach dropped, and she reminded herself of the eternity she had to grow it back. Not to mention she awas going on a humanitarian mission. The last thing she needed to be worried about was her vanity. Still, she closed her eyes as the hairdressing demon held up a mirror. When she opened them, Kat was both relieved, and a tad horrified.

Relieved because she was now positive, no one would recognize her. Horrified, because what she wore on her head was the most frightening thing she had ever seen in a mirror.

Her hair was now platinum blond. Which wouldn't have been so bad, but it was cut short in the back, with a shock of bangs that hung in front of one eye.

"Well fuck me sideways. I look like I'm going to not just demand to speak to the manager but file a formal complaint *and* write a bad Google review."

Satan was still laughing, and Kat thought she might have to rethink her previous assessment that he was a kind gentle kind of dude. He seemed to have a sadistic streak. But he was Satan after all.

In between guffaws Satan said, "It will grow back in no time. But it's really perfect. You look like you're on your way to sell diet pills at a PTA meeting," he was doubled over now. Kat hoped his sides hurt. "Maybe do a little recruiting for your MLM? You'll fit right in."

Bobby was smiling proudly behind the mirror and Kat made him put it down. She hoped this whole mission went quickly. But she had to concede that the big guy was right. She didn't look like the trouble making stripper that she had been in Heaven. Good thing Heaven was full of assholes, she really would fit right in.

"When I got to Heaven the first time, I looked like an airbrushed version of myself. But not at the gates before I got in, how do we know that I'll go through the portal and still look like this?"

"We don't," Satan said simply.

"When Amon appeared through the portal he looked like a hairy assed dog demon, not what he looks like here."

"It's true that heaven distorts physical appearance, for better or for worse. In Amon's case, he was a demon. You are, or were, human. I'd love to tell you for sure, but the truth is, I really don't know. I'm not in the business of making shit up in lieu of real answers."

While she appreciated Satan's ability to simply admit that he just didn't know, Kat was once again rethinking this whole thing.

5

Before she left, Satan told her where she could find the portal in the morning. Naturally it would be next to the lake of fire. Kat wished he had picked another lake in Hell. Any other one would have been cool. Or cooler. The lake of fire was abhorrent. The other lakes were much more pleasant. Until then, she would go home and try and relax. A task that might prove difficult. She passed Amon's house again and considered stopping, but she already had two upset cats. She didn't want an upset demon boyfriend also. She thought he wouldn't want her to go. They had talked about it many times. She thought he might be really pissed when he found out, but she figured she could smooth it out later. Hell had drastically improved her fellatio skills, and those might just come in handy.

She walked carefully as she passed Amon's house just in case, he was home and might stop her as she walked by. She felt guilty. But not for long, as she saw Amon walking towards her. The look on his face when he saw her was one of horror.

"I'm sorry," Kat said to Amon's dropped jaw. "I was going to tell you...I promise."

"Oh no, you wouldn't have had to. Your hair speaks for itself. You really didn't need to do all that. You know you could have just said you needed some space," Amon said. "I wouldn't have recognized you if it weren't for the fact that you're wearing my shirt."

Kat looked at him sideways, Amon was a smart guy, but she didn't think he had yet to connect her new do with her going to do Satan's bidding. She also made a mental note not to wear an old T-shirt to Heaven. She was going to need to find a robe like they wore up there. She shuddered at the thought of the glittery fashion fail.

"I'm sorry, it will grow back I promise," Kat said.

"Well, let's hope whoever did that to you gets what's coming," Amon said, still staring at her head. He reached up and touched her stiff blow-dried bangs. "That's really something. Did you piss someone off?"

Kat was getting frustrated now, and a little offended too. It was bad, but it couldn't warrant this kind of abuse. But she didn't see how she could hide the reason for the nightmare on her head. It would be one thing to sneak off before she had talked to him. Another to lie to his face.

"I've agreed to go back to Heaven," Kat said and winced. "Just for a little while, and just to rescue some souls."

Amon looked a little dazed, but not too upset. "I hate that idea. But I will support your decision. And bringing back good souls shouldn't be too dangerous. It's not like you're trying to get the real dicks back to Hell. Then I would be really nervous."

Kat cringed. "Uh... yeah, that would be really dangerous."

"You're going to try and get a few of the baddies too, aren't you?" Amon scowled. When she had first met him in Heaven, that scowl would have scared the BeJesus out of her. He looked like some sort of evil canine thing. Here in Hell, he was much cuter. Hot even. With his blond crew cut and red tinted beard, "God isn't going to give a shit about the regular souls in Heaven. But the redeemed are going to be a different story all together."

She hadn't thought about that, but it made sense. The whole point of Heaven was that anyone could get there if they repented and accepted God. The mass murderers, spree killers, and people who never returned their grocery carts to the corrals would be God's special ones. The ones that proved His mercy.

"Yeah, but you know, fuck them. If I'm doing this, I'm doing it. I'm not going to half ass it," Kat started laughing as she wouldn't have a butthole in Heaven. She wasn't likely to have half an ass let alone a whole one.

Amon grabbed her and kissed her hard.

"You know that's why I love you. You're such a badass. A whole badass."

He let her go and they turned and started walking back to his place.

"How about you help me get ready?" She asked.

"I just wish I could go with you, but you know how I get when I cross into Heaven."

Kat knew. It wasn't pretty, it was horrific.

"Did it hurt?"

"Heaven? Hell, yes it hurt. But I'm guessing Satan wouldn't be sending you if you would have that same problem. You're a human soul; your appearance won't change. That is the reason behind that thing on your head, right?"

It was the reason, but she didn't want to tell him that Satan wasn't sure if it would hold or not. For all she knew, she could go back to her angelic self or become a hideous fire burping demon like the love of her life had. Or in this case, the love of her death.

They reached Amon's house, and he unlocked the door. She stepped inside his cozy little abode. The furniture was worn like hers, but it was comfortable. He slipped into the kitchen while she waited, and she heard the microwave running. He came back with a box of not quite stale chocolate donuts and two nuked mugs of tea. The only way to make tea in Hell was in the microwave.

She sipped her tea in silence. She pondered a donut as she watched Amon take a large bite but found she didn't have the appetite for it.

"You know, maybe while you're there, I can come check on you," Amon said after swallowing.

"And perhaps get you a piece of Heaven fruit for your troubles? Since I'll be there anyway, right?"

Amon smiled.

"I mean that would be cool."

"I really think I need to do this. Satan says he will have my back, and I trust him."

"If he said that, he means it. I don't want you to go. Hell is much better with you in it. But I get it. It's not just that you're a badass, Kat, it's that you give a shit. You could just say no and call it good. But that's not you."

She didn't know what to say to that, so she leaned in and kissed him. Of all the guys, which was quite a few, it took a damned demon to make her fall in love. It didn't take long before the kissing turned into much more. Her T-shirt hit the floor, and she climbed on top of him. Determined to make the most of this time before she went back to Heaven and lost her genitals again. God had fixed the glitch that made it possible for her and everyone else's, sexy bits to come back. It seems that orgies, even of the angelic type, are frowned upon in Heaven.

Panting she laid back in his arms, and they cuddled. She hated cuddling on earth. She was a master at leaving her suitors in their beds, wondering what had happened and sometimes where she had gone. One time, she had wriggled out of a bathroom window in her underwear to avoid this very thing. But now she loved it. With him she loved it, and even after all that had happened it surprised her. The next thing she knew, she'd be watching romcoms and planning weddings.

"I have to find a robe," she said, reluctantly breaking the silence.

"I think I know where we can find one." He paused, "I have just the thing actually."

He peeled himself away, leaving her to shiver at the loss of his warmth. He trotted into his bedroom before trotting back holding a silver glittering robe his demon member bobbing up and down with his steps. He held up the robe, and it looked a lot like what they wore in Heaven. In fact, it looked like the very robe that Lyla had been wearing when Kat grabbed her and brought her to Hell. Kat had tossed hers into the lake of fire.

"It's Lyla's. She was going to throw it away, but I kept it. It's kind of beat up."

That was putting it mildly. The thing had a hole in it and was filthy. Kat wasn't all that surprised that he had kept it. Amon was a bit of a pack rat. A hoarder if she were honest. It was kind of obvious when you stepped into his house. It was packed full. Neatly, but full of stuff. He had this thing about throwing things away, especially if he thought he could find a use for it.

"Maybe we can fix it?"

"I think we can. I have a sewing machine someone lost in a bet. I've learned to do a couple of things. Basic stuff. Here try it on."

He handed the beat-up angel robe to her, and she slipped it over her head with a grimace.

"Ugh…it stinks."

"I'll bet. Our friend had a bit of an accident on her way down," he cringed. "Let me just look at what I can do then we'll wash it."

He looked at her up and down, then stuck his finger in the tear at the front of the robe. It was huge on her, but she was happy for that. It would need to be taken in, but for now it allowed her to kind of avoid most of the fouled fabric from touching her skin. He read her thoughts, and whisked the dirty thing off of her, and disappeared into the back of the house where she heard a thump and the sound of the washing machine.

"We'll run it twice. The hole will be easy, and I can take it in. You'll look like an asshole, it will be perfect," he grinned. "I'll make some dinner."

Amon left her with a fresh bowl in his pipe, and a rerun of Jeopardy on the TV while he went into his kitchen. She had seen this episode but hadn't memorized the answers. She yelled her responses at the TV. Getting most of them wrong. Amon returned with two plates of slightly overcooked pasta, he came back with a bottle of mid-range wine and two wine glasses, one of them chipped. He poured the wine, taking the chipped glass for himself. He lifted his glass to her, and she lifted hers.

"A toast to my favorite fallen angel."They clinked glasses and sipped.

After they ate, Amon got the robe out of the dryer and patched the hole in it, before downsizing it considerably. She tried it on and looked in the mirror.

"You look awful," Amon said and raised his glass to salute her before draining it.

Kat stared at her reflection with wide eyes, then drained her own glass.

"I guess this will do. I got to get back to feed my damned cats. Oh, and I guess I should ask you if you would mind looking after them while I'm gone?"

"Of course. I'll walk you back."

She changed into her, once his, T shirt and worn-out jeans, and they walked in silence back to her house. Her two damned cats were waiting for her on the sofa, as she stepped through the door. Lucifer jumped off the couch, presented his ass and slunk into the bedroom. Buster gave her a look of disgust and put his head down. She thought he was going to sleep, but he kept one eye open to continue his dirty look.

"I guess they're not pleased you're going either," Amon said.

"It appears that way. I hope I'm not doing something really stupid. I've got a good thing going here in hell," Kat pulled him toward the bedroom. "I don't want to fuck it up."

"I think it will be ok, you have Satan on your side. And I can come check on you through the portal. You won't be alone."

They made it into the bedroom and onto the bed, where Lucifer had gone to sulk. He hopped down and joined Buster on the couch. Kat just shook her head and climbed into bed with Amon. He was a horny little demon, despite not having any horns. They had sex one last time before falling asleep.

He was gone when she woke the next morning. She thought she had closed the curtains before bed, but Hell's sun shined through her window. Lucifer and Buster had replaced her demon, and while she was happy about that she was bummed to not wake up with Amon. Then she smelled the coffee. She got up, careful not to disturb the felines, and went into her kitchen to find a naked Amon holding two steaming mugs of mediocre coffee.

"You're up! Your cats usurped my place in your bed, so I thought I would make some coffee," he said.

She took her mug and smiled at him.

"Well, I suppose I'm really doing this."

"You kind of have to now. I mean, you're not going to get invited to any orgies with that haircut. Might as well make use of it until it grows back."

"Right? Well, let's get to it."

She grabbed her robe and slipped it over her head. Amon got dressed too and they were about to head out when Lucifer jumped into her arms.

"Kat! Please don't go. Please," the little furball looked at her with panicked eyes and attached himself to her legs.

6

It took her a whole five minutes to dislodge Lucifer from her legs. And another five minutes before she had reassured him and placed him next to her other pissed off cat. When they were finally able to leave, Amon and Kat stepped out into the bright, or bright-ish, morning in Hell. The sun was shining through a veil of red mist that gave the whole place a deep crimson glow. The previous rainstorm had left the place nourished. They were silent as they walked to where the new portal was supposed to be.

Kat wished the Lake of Fire wasn't as close as it was, and they were there in less than ten minutes. The winged demons swooped and swirled over the molten lake. Occasionally they dipped down and touched it, setting their wings alight before darting back up into the sky. It appeared to Kat to be some sort of game. As she looked out at the dark rocky hills and black sand that surrounded the lake, she wondered why she had thought it was so bad before. Then she remembered the charred living corpses she had seen the last time. But without that, it was almost pleasant.

Satan waved to her and Amon as they approached the lake. He had laid out a picnic blanket out on the sand, laden with pastries and fruit and coffee. He looked at her and doubled over laughing.

He spoke between labored breaths, "Oh my Lemmy, you look God awful. It's fucking perfect," he kept laughing.

"Thanks," Kat frowned.

"Where on earth did you get that robe?"

"I kept it when Lyla came down, so not earth, but Heaven." Amon replied stifling his own snicker, Kat elbowed him hard in the ribs. "Ow," he said through a giggle.

"Here sit a minute and enjoy, Heaven can wait," Satan said.

They sat and Satan poured them both a cup of coffee. It tasted brewed and not instant. Kat was impressed. She nibbled on a pastry. Amon picked up a donut and an orange slice which he bit into with a grimace.

"Yeah, I know, I will try and get some fruit for you when you come to check on me," Amon said nothing and just smiled.

"So, are you ready? Do you have a game plan?" Satan asked through a mouthful of cheese Danish.

"I'm thinking I'm going to go to my dad's house first. He should be able to help me figure it all out," Kat thought he was her best bet. He had died when she was so young, and she knew from her first encounter with him in Heaven that he would be happy to help her. If she could get him sober. They had both missed out on having a relationship when they were alive. Tears stung her eyes as she thought about it. She didn't have the chance to bring him with her when she had escaped Heaven, but he seemed open to reason, unlike her aunt Judy. Judy was terrified beyond reason of God and his angels. But Kat's determination came with a side of optimism, so she thought she would give it another try if she had the chance.

As she ate, Kat saw a little bunny hopping around on the sand. She held out a piece of fruit, and it came closer. Not as apprehensive as an earth bunny might have been. She thought the sharp fangs and claws had a lot to do with their bravery. When you're little, you got to be tough she figured. It took the fruit out of her hand and allowed her to pet its head. It nuzzled against her hand, before hopping away. The animals in hell were mostly friendly. It made her not feel all that bad for those who got dipped in the lake for being mean to them. Fangs and claws aside, they were still pretty cute. Even Satan's minions had their charms.

When they finished eating, Satan snapped his fingers and one of his demon minions packed up what was left. He motioned for them to follow him, and he led them to a pile of rocks near the edge of the burning lake. It looked similar to the rocks that hid the portal in Heaven, except that it lacked soft grass, a rainbow waterfall, and heaven fruit trees.

"Here it is. Just step through and you'll come out into Heaven. I can't say where exactly, but it will get you there," Satan said, his voice taking that unnerving tone.

"The trip down was rough, will it be like that?" Kat said, not bothering to mask the anxiety in her voice.

"I don't think so. Your trip here was one of a kind."

"Going through for me was just a little bit of a hike, I think it will be like that. I can come with you if you want me to," Amon said.

"I think that will be nice actually, if it's all good with you," She asked Satan.

"Of course, I think that's a splendid idea." Satan extended his hand to Amon, who took it. He shook it vigorously, "Glad she has you, buddy. A match made in Hell." Satan didn't grab Kat's hand but lifted all of her off the ground and enveloped her into his arms. He swung her back and forth, she struggled to breathe, until he loosened his grip and let her down.

The portal looked like the mouth of Hell and definitely not a tunnel to Heaven. A black yawning maw that smelled vaguely of sulfur and oddly, gardenia. Kat wasn't as anxious as she thought she would be at the thought of entering this dark hole. Living in Hell had some surprising advantages, not the least of which included not being as scared of things that would have freaked her the fuck out on earth. Bunnies with fangs, demons playing soccer with severed heads, and blood rain had changed her perspective on just what exactly was worth being afraid of. Most of it was about as scary as walking through a Halloween store. What really stoked her fear were Jesus, God, and the angels she might encounter on the other side. The real monsters.

Amon entered first, and as Kat followed him, she felt the sting of Satan's hand slapping her ass.

"Give 'em Hell Kat!" He shouted after them, his voice echoed off the walls of the portal.

It was dark, but not too dark to see. The soft flickering of candlelight allowed them to see enough to be confident that they wouldn't trip and fall on their faces. Kat looked closer at one of them and saw it was a Gardenia scented candle with the brand name Blood Bath and Beyond. She smiled as she thought of Satan remembering her favorite flower.

The portal was cool enough to bring goosebumps to her skin. She could hear things moving on the ceiling, but it was too high for her to see how far away they were. They didn't scare her though, as they were from hell and on her side. Hell-bats maybe. The thought brought her comfort. Amon held her hand but didn't speak as they walked. It wasn't long before a hideous light appeared at what must be the entrance to heaven. The goosebumps that had retreated as she grew accustomed to the temperature, reemerged.

"Welp, were here," Amon said. "This is where I let you go. Toss a rock through when you need me. I'll keep a look out."

She took off the dirty sneakers she had been wearing as shoes weren't necessary in Heaven and handed them to Amon. He put one close to his mouth as if to lick it, then smiled as she laughed. He then turned to hug her, his hands slowly moving to squeeze her ass through Lyla's glittery robe. She kissed him for much too long, and he had to push her away to break free. Kat turned toward the light and away from him. She felt nauseous as she stepped into the blinding glow.

To her surprise, the nausea stayed with her as she entered Heaven. The portal was hidden by an outcropping of rocks, but there was no lake or waterfall. Just soft grass in the middle of a grouping of fruit trees. The orange fruit that hung on them looked like they were about to burst. She knew that each one would be perfectly ripe and juicy. Finding an imperfect piece of fruit would be impossible here. Part of her wanted to grab one and stuff it in her face, but most of her resented its perfection. She knew she would give in at some point, but spite made her refrain for the moment.

She actually felt like shit, she knew she looked like shit, but she was supposed to look like shit. She hadn't expected to feel pain, but her back and arm hurt. She was unstable as she walked. Kat figured that must be a consequence of coming back here. It wasn't intolerable though and she thought she could power through it.

She stepped into the greenery and heard the birds and squirrels doing their thing in the trees. She also heard someone softly humming a tune nearby. She thought it sounded vaguely like Taylor Swift, which dispelled any lingering doubts she might have had that she was in Heaven. Better than Nickelback, but still horrific enough for Heaven. Her instincts told her to run the other way, but the sound moved her in its direction despite her better judgment. For all she knew it could be one of the dick angels or fuck… even Hitler himself. But still she found the sound intoxicating and was compelled to see who or what it was coming from.

Her legs and whole body just felt so weird, and she had to focus intently on each step to stay upright. She figured it might be like getting your sea legs on a boat, she would adjust if she just kept trying, so that's what she did. And each step became just a bit easier. Not far in the distance, she saw a figure sitting in a field of flowers. She saw the back of a women, wingless, and with flaming red hair. A halo sparkled in the sun on top of her head. She was facing an easel and a blank canvas. More canvases lay around her on the ground. Each appeared to be finished. She hadn't noticed Kat creeping up behind her, and Kat wanted it that way. She wanted to watch the woman for a while before she decided whether to approach her or not.

The woman raised her hand holding a paintbrush, a palate sat on her lap. She was about to touch the brush to the empty canvas, when the humming stopped, and the lady said quietly, "Fuck."

It was almost a whisper, but Kat still heard it and cocked her head. Was this lady frustrated? The finished paintings on the ground were nothing short of breathtaking. Animals, landscapes, and portraits of angels surrounded her. Each was more beautiful than the last. And then Kat knew what was probably bothering this woman. She must have been an artist on earth. This was art without the challenge of creation. It was not and probably could not be a genuine reflection of humanity. Kat didn't think art could be art, if it lacked its human qualities. What a nightmare it must be for the artist to find that in heaven, their talent was negated. A rare talent rendered irrelevant.

She watched for a few more minutes, working up the nerve to approach her. But the more she watched, the more she sympathized with the frustrated artist. Kat thought they might be kindred spirits despite the utterly offensive tune she had been humming. As she looked at the back of the woman's head, her hand that held the paintbrush now lying still in her lap, Kat felt blessed by Satan. This was the exact soul she had been sent here to retrieve. The one that understood that the paradise sold in church was a deception. True peace and contentment did not come from a life free of effort. Heaven was an empty, vapid, and selfish place underneath the sparkles and sprinkled donuts. She hadn't wanted to have to convince anyone of that. She didn't want to be that chick, the chick that forced knowledge on those that didn't ask for it. This lady had already figured it out. She may not know that the place where she could find real peace was in Hell, but she might have realized that Heaven wasn't what it wanted her to believe. That was plenty for Kat.

Kat took a deep breath, which was uncomfortable, and as she let it out, she said, "Hello…" she meant to say more but the sound of her voice stopped her cold. It was odd, maybe a little gravelly, but not normal. She pondered this and was about to try again, but the woman turned around to look at her and screamed.

7

The redhaired lady put a fist in her mouth to stifle her scream. Kat was annoyed. She knew her haircut was awful, but this seemed like a gross over reaction. Mean even. She began to think that maybe her first impression that this lady was her kindred spirit was a little premature. This lady might just be another shallow judgy angel. Although, the look on her face had morphed from fear to concern, and that development puzzled Kat. She lifted her hand to her hair, meaning to try and pat down her hair sprayed bangs, and saw the bone sticking out of her bloody arm. It was then that she also noticed the glitter that dotted her bruised and bloodied skin. It wasn't the heavenly glitter that was embedded in just about everything, but the kind that infested the strip club. This poor lady wasn't scared of her haircut, nor had Kat appeared as a demon like Amon had. No, Kat showed up to Heaven as she had at the pearly gates. Fresh from the car wreck that took her, and her cat's lives. She looked like an un-showered, strippery, glittery nightmare.

"It's ok, I'm just dead…like you," Kat smiled and tried to extend a hand before she remembered the grievous injury to her arm. Her right hand just hung there limply. She took her dangling hand with her good one and yanked hard, hoping to set the bone in a less alarming way. "Son of a fucking bitch…" She yelped.

"Uh… let me help you. Or try at least," the woman said.

The lady took Kat's broken arm, and pulled gently, extending the arm delicately. The bone slid back under the skin of her arm. They both sucked air through their teeth with a hiss as it did. Kat ground her teeth together in an attempt to hide how much it hurt, remembering that there wasn't supposed to be any pain in Heaven. She realized by the look on the woman's face that she had failed.

"I'm so sorry. You must be in pain, but I don't understand how," she said.

"God hates me, I suspect he hates us all." Kat replied, then cringed when she saw the lady cock her head to the side like a confused puppy. "I'm Kat. And what I meant to say, is this is how I died. It doesn't hurt that bad. Barely at all." Kat tried to smile, hoping that would hide her very obvious lie. The look on the other lady's face told her she had failed again.

"Uh…I'm Jesseca but call me Jess." she extended her hand then retracted it quickly. "Here why don't you sit down?" Jesseca motioned to the chair next to her easel.

Kat moved carefully to the chair, trying to walk like her spine wasn't broken. She was mostly successful. She sat down, then leaned awkwardly to the side. She put a hand on the ground and pushed off, trying to balance herself upright and into a seated position.

"I think we should get you to the Administration building, I'm sure someone there can fix you up. I'm sure God doesn't hate you Kat, this must be some kind of mistake."

"I thought God doesn't make mistakes…" Kat said.

Jess pondered this idea, "You're right. This is really weird though. I haven't been here all that long, but I didn't think pain or injury was a thing in Heaven." She paused, "Or any kind of bad feeling." She sounded more like she was asking a question rather than stating a fact.

"But you looked upset just now. That was why I came over," Kat said.

Jess sighed, "I was, am. My paintings up here, aren't quite turning out as I wanted…" she looked puzzled again. "Not that I'm not grateful, but they are all so perfect…." A glimmer of frown grew on her face, but only for a moment, as Jess forced it away with a manufactured smile.

"They're all beautiful," Kat said.

"I know, and like I said, I'm so grateful. God is so good…" she looked down. "But…they weren't like this on earth. They weren't perfect. People liked them, I liked them. But they weren't perfect. My paintings now feel…like they were generated by a computer, not a human. It's like they're made by a robot."

"Fake?"

Jess sighed again, and that phantom frown appeared again, briefly. She looked up again at Kat and said, "We should really get you some help. Why don't you stay here, and I'll go get someone?"

"No. I know it sounds weird. But they must want me this way."

"Kat, that just can't be. This is Heaven. I know there shouldn't be mistakes here but maybe shit happens. You know, like on earth?"

"Or maybe things here aren't quite what they seem?"

Jess didn't try to fight her frown now, and Kat saw the shimmer of tears in her deep blue eyes. "I've thought that for a while now. Some things just seem wrong," her voice was a troubled whisper. "Do you think this could be Hell? Like I screwed up somehow and part of my punishment is to make me think I made it to Heaven? Purgatory maybe?" If Heaven had allowed tears to fall, they would be running down her cute lightly freckled cheeks. The sadness in her eyes brought tears to Kat's eyes too.

"No, Jess. It's not. I promise. But your instincts are right. Things are not what they seem."

"There's something not right, but you're the first person I've been able to say that too. Everyone here just seems to be so happy, but my gut says they might not be. And they all seem just a little afraid."

The more they talked, the more she felt connected to this confused soul in Heaven. Despite the Taylor Swift song. Maybe it was the artist thing, the creative part of her. She had recognized the fear in the other angels, the fear that wouldn't allow Aunt Judy to hear her when she told her about Hell. This lady was exactly who she was hoping to meet and possibly take back to Hell. But she wasn't quite sure how to start the conversation. She decided she would try lead her to her own conclusion, rather than drop the whole Satan is cool and Hell is awesome thing on her. Ease her into coming to that idea on her own.

"Afraid how?" Kat asked gently, still trying to stay upright in her chair.

"Well, like someone is listening maybe…? Or that if they say something critical, they could…I don't know…. get thrown out?"

"Trust me, it's hard as fuck to get thrown out of Heaven…"

Jess gave her the confused puppy dog head cock again, "Really?"

Kat stammered, "What I meant was, once you're here you're here right? Isn't that the whole point of salvation?"

"I guess so, but what else would they be afraid of? Something just feels wrong here. You really don't think this could be purgatory? I mean, all the stuff that is supposed to be perfect, is perfect, but it sucks the fun out of it. Honestly, it's kind of boring."

She's getting closer, Kat thought. "Have you made any friends here or met any relatives?"

"Not really. They were kind of cold, they didn't remember much. My own memories are fading too. I'm not sure how long I've been here, but I'm starting to forget. And no one wants to give me a straight answer about anything. And as far as the others, I just don't seem to fit in here. As weird as that sounds."

"Are you happy here?"

"Of course, it's Heaven. Considering the alternative…" anxiety crept into her voice.

Kat had a choice here; did she tell her about the lie that was Heaven? That all the scary shit about Satan and Hell was just God's propaganda campaign? She might sound like she was trying to sell her a tin foil hat or something.

"What if Satan turned to out to be the good guy?" Kat took a chance.

Jess cocked her head again, and turned the tables on her, "Why do you think they wouldn't help you? You kind of glossed over that, but I have a feeling it's important." Kat liked her even more; this lady was a smart one.

"Ok, so I'm just going to lay it all out there. Maybe you'll find the straight dope refreshing. I know exactly what you are going through. Well, maybe not exactly, but I get it I promise."

"I'm intrigued at least…" she said.

"So, I wasn't the greatest person on earth, to put it mildly. And on top of that I was an unbeliever. But when I knew I was dying, I repented and promised to love God and all that jazz. I was more surprised than St Peter that I got in I swear. I figured I was going to Hell. I was relieved that I made it in, at least for a little while. But then, like you, I started to notice some fucked up stuff. Like my neighbor was Jeffery Dahmer…"

"Who?" Jess interrupted.

"A serial killer who ate people," Kat replied and then wondered just how she'd been dead.

"Oh," she cringed. "I guess he repented then?"

"Yup, and trust me, he's not even the worst dude here, by a lot. So long story short, I ended up meeting a demon through a portal from Hell. Sweet guy I swear, and he had weed."

"Oh god, how I miss pot," Jess mused. "And sex, while we're on the subject."

"Right? I did too. Any who, he told me about Hell and how it isn't what I had thought it was. The weather is pretty warm, sure, but it's honest. And the whole burning forever, isn't really a thing. Unless you're a real asshole. And not the run of the mill kind of asshole that maybe drives a BMW or something. But the real fuckheads, like mass murderers and stuff." Kat wondered if she might be losing her, so she added really quick, "And there's sex there. And cats. All the cats."

"Echo?" Tears stood in her eyes again. "I mean dogs are cool too, but I miss my cat."

"Dude, I know."

Curiosity replaced her tears, "Did you go to Hell?"

"Yup. I escaped through a portal. Hell is awesome. I swear. Satan is so sweet. That portal was destroyed. But they made a new one. Einstein made a new one. That's how I got here now. Although obviously, there are some flaws. I didn't know I would end up like I did when I died. But I'm here to help find people like me. Or people like you really."

Jess looked skeptical, "How do I know you're telling me the truth though?"

"That's an honest, not to mention smart, question. I doubted Amon, the demon too. Now he's my boyfriend," Kat didn't think that helped much. And what could she do really to prove that Hell wasn't the horror show it was made out to be. Maybe it was a horror show, but not like Heaven was. "I could show you the portal?"

"Sure, I'm not sure how that will help, but I'll take a look."

Kat tried to stand on her own, but Jess wouldn't let her. She took her good hand, helped her stand and walk toward the portal.

"I guess I don't know how to show you that I'm telling the truth here."

"I mean, isn't Satan the father of Lies?"

"That's the thing though, he's really not. He's a little hard to look at for sure, but for real, he's honest. Not like God. And if he doesn't know something, he says so. He doesn't make shit up. Have you ever asked where your cat went?"

"I did."

"And…...?"

"I never got a straight answer. They just wanted to replace her, but I refused. You say all cats go to Hell?"

"They do. And God made it that way."

"What a dick."

"That's what I'm saying. He's not the benevolent being he makes himself out to be. Most of the scientists are there too. The people who made things better, for the most part at least, on earth are in Hell for fuck's sake."

"I was wondering that when you said Einstein made the portal."

They reached the rocks at the entrance to the portal to Hell. Jess let Kat go, and Kat stepped into the dark space. Her body was healed as she entered. She turned to look at Jess with her uninjured arms to show her that she was whole again.

"See, I'm all better. She lifted her robe to show that she was in fact all the way intact."

Jess cringed, "That haircut though. Satan can't be the good guy if he did that to you."

8

Kat reached up with her now healed, but scarred arm and felt the three cans of aqua net that held her horrific bangs in place. She frowned at who she hoped was a new friend.

"He did this to protect me. Or one of his demons did. So, word to the wise, find a used-to-be human hairdresser and not one born of the flames of Hell. It will grow back," Kat said, trying and ultimately failing to keep the irritation from her voice.

"Sorry, I didn't mean to be mean," Jess said. "Some of the angels can be real jerks like that, one of them made fun of my freckles. And not in a nice way, like pretending to be nice, but definitely not. Like in a 'you can't ever be one of the cool kids' kind of way. Heaven can get pretty lonely."

"Trust me I get it, that's one of the first things that made me want to get out," Kat said. "I guess I'm not surprised that you haven't heard of me. They probably kept that on the down low. But I know, and you probably shouldn't trust me just yet, so how about this? I'll go check in with the big boss and see what I can do about the whole my being bloody and broken thing in Heaven. I'll come back tomorrow and bring you some weed. I can check on you cat too."

"I'd appreciate that," Jess said. "Are you sure you're ok though?"

"I am. Just need to figure out some logistics, I think. I'm kind of blazing a new trail here." Kat reached her right hand through the opening to shake her hand one more time, but the hand dangled from her broken arm again. "Sorry, I don't think I'm going to get used to that. I'll catch you tomorrow. Lovely to meet you."

Jess nodded, and Kat turned to walk back to Hell. She was wondering just what to do. The gardenia candles lit up as she walked past them. The entrance on the other side was empty. Except for the flying bird demons, who were still doing their thing in the air. They were actually kind of cool. Kat wondered if Jess might like to paint them. When she was alive, she might have thought the whole scene hideous, but it really wasn't. It was rather majestic. When she returned her gaze from the sky to the road, she saw Satan walking toward her.

"Hey Kat! I was just coming to meet you. I heard you coming back. You, ok? How did it go?"

"You heard?"

"Yeah, like Amon heard you tossing the rocks, I get a notification when there's movement in the tunnel. You weren't gone very long." He turned to walk with her, she assumed back to her place where she expected Amon to be waiting with her perturbed felines.

"So, I'm all broken and bloody there now. I doubt I'll be able complete my mission in that condition. But I did meet someone who might listen to me. She's an artist. Really nice, smart too. She knows something sketchy is up there. A Taylor Swift fan though…."

"Eeeewwww, but hey still not deserving of Heaven," he laughed. "And still not as bad as that haircut." He put a huge hand on her head and ruffled her shortish blond hair. "Here let me fix that for you." He grinned at her when he took his hand away.

A lock of brown hair fell in front of her eyes, and she blew it away. Then looked at the Father of Lies himself and scowled.

"What the fuck?"

Satan was laughing. Then doubled over laughing, then rolled on the ground laughing. As Kat watched the huge red beast, this monster who ruled in Hell, roll around on the ground like a child, mudding up his purple velour jumpsuit, she started laughing in spite of herself.

"What is so funny?" Amon asked, Kat hadn't noticed his approach. "And Kat, wow that's way better."

"I got her so gooood!" Satan said, between giggles. "But in my defense, I thought it might have a better chance of staying like that if we did it analog."

Kat wanted to be mad, but between the laughter and the relief that she wouldn't have to wait to grow her hair out, she really wasn't.

"So, for real, how the fuck am I supposed to convince people you're not the Great Deceiver when you're going to pull shit like that?" It occurred to her that chastising Satan might be a bad idea, but then again, she had shit talked St Peter and God himself. Satan was a kitten compared to those two.

Satan gave her a sheepish shrug, "So let's head back to my place, I'll get us some dinner and we can think this through. I'm assuming you're still willing Kat?"

"Of course, I am," she said with yet another scowl.

Satan clapped his hands and a few seconds later, two minions showed up with a large black and purple Rikshaw. Kat and Amon climbed up onto the velveteen covered seats and sat on either side of the big red guy. Velour and velveteen seemed to be the most prevalent fabrics in Hell, kind of like the strip club. And only a few minutes later they were in front of his mansion. Two more minions, looked to be preparing to shove a large wooden stake up the ass of a guy lying pleading on the ground. Kat looked at Satan and cringed.

"That's Vlad. Trust me, he earned all that. Forever."

"Vlad?"

"You know Dracula. Vlad the Impaler, Romanian asshat extraordinaire. He was Catholic, but God made an exception and sent him here. I'm thinking the optics of letting this fucker do his thing up there wouldn't suit God's propaganda agenda."

"But Hitler though…"

"Come on, what side do you think the Catholics were on anyway?" Satan rolled his eyes. "We wouldn't be here if all this were really about good and evil now, would we? Evil is about what hurts God's ego, not what actually hurts."

"Why else would He get rid of all the weed in Heaven. The bastard," Amon chimed in.

Vlad screamed as he was hoisted into the air. The minions pulling the rikshaw giggled. Kat couldn't look anymore. The blood rushed down the wooden post. She didn't feel bad for the guy, she remembered the story of Vlad the Impaler. But that didn't detract from the abject horror of it. She was surprised that he screamed like a girl though, while not surprised that he couldn't handle what he had dished out.

They dismounted, and the two minions pulled the rikshaw around the back of the mansion. Kat and Amon followed Satan up the steps to his enormous front doors, which opened as they approached, he bowed and waved them through the doors first. The doors closed with a soft woosh after Satan walked through them. He led them between the two staircases in the foyer and into a large dining room. More portraits like the one of Lemmy upstairs lined the walls. Kat recognized them all. Mark Twain, Clarence Darrow, Katherine Hepburn, the amazing James Randi, it was like the walk of fame for famous unbelievers. Satan had already taken his seat at the head of a long black dining table. Kat sat on one side and Amon took his seat at the other.

"I hope you're hungry," Satan said, as his minions began to enter the room, each holding a silver domed platter. "I had them whip up a little something. Or maybe a lot of something."

Kat hadn't thought she was hungry, but the smell that accompanied the minions made her mouth water. As they set their platters down, each minion removed the covers and bowed as they left the room. Roast beef, chicken, potatoes, ham, and even some vegetables, the array was staggering. Kat wondered how they would eat all of it. But soon she didn't have to, every minion returned wearing black bow ties. They filled the rest of the table and looked to Satan expectantly. Kat thought there must be fifty of them.

Satan turned to Kat and said, "No one eats until we say grace." Kat scrunched her eyebrows together at this but closed her eyes and bowed her head.

"Fuck it, let's eat!" Satan cried.

The minions all began to pass the platters around and to Kat's surprise, which was pretty much her default emotion in death, the minions had exceptional table manners.

As Kat filled her plate, Satan addressed the whole table, "Seriously, I wish to thank everyone her for their help and service. I love you all." He watched them with a smile for a moment, and when everyone else had gotten their plates, began to fill his own. Kat looked at him in wonder, before taking a large forkful of mashed potatoes and stuffing it into her mouth. They were delicious. And she was surprised yet again.

"Ok now to talk turkey," Satan said with a grin, holding a giant turkey leg. "So, you know I can change your looks here in Hell. But I can't really control what happens in Heaven. I have very little if any power there. I can't say that I expected that you would end up in your death body though. How bad was it?"

Kat chewed her roast beef and swallowed, "It was pretty bad. My arm and back were broken, not to mention I still had the glitter on me from work the night before. No way I can get around like that in Heaven. I'm lucky that the lady I met didn't totally freak out."

"Glitter?" Satan asked around a bite of greasy turkey meat, his manners weren't quite as good as his demons.

"I was a stripper in life."

"Groovy!" Satan sprayed her with turkey bits, and she cringed. Satan wiped her face with his napkin. "So sorry, I've been meaning to work on that," he gave her a hideously sheepish smile.

"Did it hurt? The closer I got into Heaven, the more it hurt," Amon said.

"Yeah, it did. But I think I could deal with it, if we could figure out how to make me not look like a glittery horror show."

"You said you met someone there?" Satan asked, and this time he waited until his mouth was empty. Kat marveled at his desire for self-improvement.

"I did, an artist. Her name is Jess."

"Maybe she could act on your behalf?" Amon asked.

"I don't think I would ask something like that. She was able to help me reset the bone in my arm though. That I can cover with the sleeve of my robe. I think the bigger problem is my back. I can barely walk. I keep trying to flop over. I would need a brace or something. And then there's my face. I don't know how I could go unrecognized."

"I think it's safe to assume that anything you take to Heaven will come out weird if it comes out at all," Amon said.

"The weed worked though," Kat said hopefully.

"It did, but I think it's also safe to assume that a few things have changed now. God is a dick but He's not stupid." Satan said.

"I promised Jess, I would bring her some weed tomorrow. Damnit. She's not convinced I'm telling the truth, and I was hoping that would help. Also, she's kind of bored and bummed, so I thought that would make a nice gift."

"You can try, but I wouldn't get my hopes up," Amon said.

"Her cat! She had a cat named Echo. I wouldn't want to bring it all the way to Heaven, but I know she would love to see her." Kat said. "That could help her see that I'm telling her the truth. And she is lonely and frustrated too, it would be nice to see her smile."

Satan smirked, "You find a girl crush?"

"Maybe, but mostly still into penis. I really liked her though."

"Ok, let's find her cat," Satan waved his hand to one of the identical demons. "Jo, when you're finished, please help me find this cat and prepare her for a visit. Also, some weed from my stash." Jo the demon, saluted Satan before returning to their plate. "In case the weed does make it through," he said to Kat.

The rest of the meal went without any other discussion of the mission. Satan explained while working his way through a huge pork rib, that the meat in Hell didn't come from live animals but grown like plants. One more example why having all the scientists was an advantage. When they were finished, Satan walked them to the door and hugged them goodbye.

"Amon, I trust you to see her off tomorrow? I hear Kissinger is about to head on down, and I'd like to greet him personally."

"I think I got it," Kat said. And she did think she had it.

9

Amon and Kat declined Satan's offer to have his minions cart them home, in favor of the walk. It was sunset, and the view in Hell was stunning. Purple and blue hues lit up the sky on the horizon like a beautiful bruise. Amon took her hand as they strolled. They passed the park where people were playing chess at stone tables, while hell bunnies frolicked in the blood-soaked grass. The hell birds were coming to roost in the trees, having tired themselves out playing their games at the lake of fire.

Amon followed her inside where her two very pissed off pussies were waiting for her. Lucifer tried to mimic his counterpart's apathetic façade but didn't last long. He leapt into her arms and nuzzled her chin.

"Kat, I missed you. You were gone forever," he said through a purr.

"I was gone like a few hours, and you lived through it," she said setting him on the couch to pet Buster, whose own apathy faded as soon as she scratched the top of his head.

"I'm going to step into the shower," Amon said.

"I'll be right there," Kat called to him from the kitchen, where she was filling both food dishes. She topped them both off with some chicken she had saved from Satan's feast. Neither one seemed particularly irritated with her anymore.

Kat hopped in the shower, where Amon was waiting. He washed her back and rinsed her hair, before kissing her deeply. She stopped him from going further, at least until they made it back to her bedroom. He took her in his arms, and this is the part where anywhere else, they would have made love. But this was Hell, so Amon demon-fucked her to sleep where she had nightmares of Heaven.

She woke up first in the morning and slipped out of bed to make the coffee. Amon was sitting up in bed with a smile when she walked in with two steaming mugs. They sipped coffee and watched the two kitties sleep at the foot of the bed. Kat heard a strange chirp coming from her telephone at the side of her bed. It was the kind she remembered as a kid with a large beige base and a rotary dial. But it didn't ring as if she was getting a phone call but chirped instead. She looked at it past Amon, confused.

"Someone tossed a rock into the portal. Your new friend?" He said.

"It must be," Kat replied. "I should get moving."

Kat threw the covers off of her and was chilled by the cool air without them. She slipped on her robe. No underwear needed. Underwear was, in Kat's opinion, useless anywhere, but even more so in Heaven. Her death body would still have her lady bits this time, but she still couldn't see any point to underwear.

Amon threw on his clothes and walked out the door with her. They walked quickly toward the portal but passed Amon's house on the way. His motorcycle was in the front yard. He got on it and started it up. Kat hiked up her robe and climbed onto the back of it, enjoying the breeze on the soon to be only pussy in Heaven. She wrapped her arms around his strong chest, and they rocketed toward the lake of fire.

A demon was waiting at the portal holding a cat carrier. A confused looking black and white cat sat inside. It had a white muzzle with a white stripe that went to the top of its forehead. The demon handed her a pouch, which she assumed had a pipe, lighter, and some of Satan's personal weed. She could smell it through the fabric.

"He's got a dick face!" Amon laughed as he petted the cat through the top of the carrier.

"It's a she, Echo. Be nice," she said. Although her markings did kind of resemble a dick.

Kat reached in the carrier to scratch between her ears. Echo pushed her head back to meet her hand and purred. They stepped into the portal and as they got close, a pebble bounced off her forehead.

"Ow…" Kat cried out.

"Sorry, Jess called back. I wasn't sure if you got the message."

"I got it," Kat said rubbing her forehead.

Amon giggled.

"Someone wants to say Hi!" Kat said as she moved toward the light of Heaven. Jess stood silhouetted in the opening.

Kat got as close to the entrance as she dared and opened the top of the carrier. She pulled out the kitty, who now seemed a little frightened. She held her close to her chest and tried to keep her calm.

"Echo?" Jess said. "Oh my god, is that really you?"

Echo made the tiniest meow.

"I have no idea what will happen if I bring her through, it might hurt her," Kat said. Jess was hopping up and down in the opening. She reached through and touched the cat but quickly withdrew. But then she stepped all the way into the portal, "Wait!" Kat cried, but it was too late. Kat didn't know what would happen when she stepped through if she would be able to get back or what. But Jess was already there, telling her that now would be pointless.

Kat handed the cat over to her. Echo no longer seemed afraid, and tears began to stream down Jess' face. She sat down on the floor of the portal with Echo in her lap. Kat and Amon just watched and smiled. The bats or whatever they were scuttled along the darkened ceiling, and Jess either didn't notice or didn't care. Her face lit only by candlelight, the look of joy and relief reinforced Kat's resolve to save as many souls as she could from the torment of God's paradise.

"I brought some weed too. Courtesy of Satan. It's from his private stash. And this is Amon, the demon I was telling you about."

"He doesn't look like a demon," Jess said.

"Only if I step through that hole, gives me wicked heartburn too.

"No shit, the dude breathed fire when we first met."

Amon packed the bowl and handed it to Jess, whose apprehension, if she had had any at all, was no longer apparent. She closed her eyes as she drew in the sweet smoke.

"Oh my…If you're trying to convince me to go to Hell, you're doing a bang-up job."

"So, for real, I'm not completely sure what will happen if you go back into Heaven. I know Echo can't come with you," Kat said.

"I think Jess will be okay Kat. The portal seems to be neutral in all this. The cat though, might be like she was when she died, like you. And that would really suck," Amon said.

The pipe went around one more time, before Amon put it back in the pouch and handed it to Jess. Echo was fast asleep in her lap.

"I don't think I want to go back," Jess said. Sadness bled through her words and Kat could see she was crying again. "I asked about you Kat. I went straight to the Administration office and asked the front desk angel."

"Chad?" Kat asked.

"No Chris, I think. He didn't tell me shit, but I could see it in his eyes. I believe you Kat. I think they probably covered it up. I've been fooling myself that I'm happy there. But Heaven kind of sucks ass. I asked about that killer, and you're right, he's there. And they got all pissy about it too. Salvation and all that. Not to mention, but my uh…you know…is back. And honestly, it feels good to cry for real."

"So, you want to come with us?" Kat asked.

"No," Jess said. "Well, yes. But not yet. I want to help." Her tears had stopped.

"Really?" Kat said.

"Yes, this is bullshit. I've been thinking about it ever since we met. I still wasn't sure after I talked to you and the angel. All of this is fucking nuts, and I wondered if you might bring me some fake cat or something. Or otherwise try to trick me, but this is Echo. I have no doubt. And even if Hell isn't paradise, and you haven't tried to convince me that it is, it's better than being lied to. So yeah, I want to help." Her tears had dried, and while Kat didn't think it was anger, she was definitely fired up.

"Thank you," Kat said. "Ok, so what do we do now?"

Jess gently removed Echo from her lap and set her on the ground where she sat and watched her deceased human quietly. Jess took a few tentative steps toward the light, and Kat heard her take a deep breath before stepping though. Kat and Amon held their own breath as the watched to see what would happen. If she would change or stay as she was. Jess turned around to face them in the portal and lifted her robe. It was as smooth as a plastic baby doll. She gave a thumbs up and checked her pocket where she had deposited the pouch Amon had given her and gave a thumbs down when she saw that her pocket was empty. She returned to the portal and sat back down, and Echo took her place back on her lap. Her halo stayed with her the whole time.

"So, I was thinking, that if it turned out that you weren't a damned liar," Jess paused for effect at her pun, "How I could help you go unnoticed in Heaven. You can't walk around as you were looking like a horror movie extra."

"It couldn't have been that bad," Kat said scrunching her eyebrows together.

"Oh yeah, it was that bad. Why do you think I thought I might be in Hell and not Heaven? The glitter was an interesting touch though.

"The glitter wasn't intentional," Kat said again.

"Oh, were you a kindergarten teacher?"

"Something like that but go on. I want to hear your idea."

"So, first we need to brace your back. The wobbly falling over thing is a problem. I thought maybe I just wish for a brace, but who knows how or if they monitor that stuff. So, I was thinking maybe a tree branch? Right? We tie it up under your robe, to secure your spine. We were able to get your arm bone back in already, and that will be disguised under your sleeve."

Smart and creative, Kat thought she really hit the jackpot. Of all the people she could have met first she me this one. And here she thought they might not get along.

"Try one of those fruit trees," Amon said. "You can bring us some of the fruit if it falls off." Kat rolled her eyes at him. He was still obsessed with that stuff.

"Um ok, sure. If all that works, we will still need to deal with your face. But I have my paints. I can totally paint you a new face. Or hide the one you have."

If this conversation had happened in any other context, Kat thought she might have socked Jess in the gut. But it all made sense.

"What about my hair?"

"I think we can try to cut it, and if it won't stay, I'll paint it too."

"Well fuck, let's give it a go. Can you go and gather what you'll need and bring it to the entrance of the portal? Then I'll come through and you can fix me up."

"And get some fruit while you're at it?" Amon said.

"I've already done that, except the fruit part," Jess said.

"I thought you said you weren't sure you believed me?"

"Meh, I wanted to be cautious, but my instincts told me you were cool from the beginning." Jess smiled and once again got up and placed Echo on the ground next to her. She grabbed Kat for a hug, "I'm a hugger. I hope you don't mind." If Kat minded the point was already moot, as she was already in her arms. "Come on."

Jess pulled Kat into the light. As soon as she was through her arm and back were broken again. But Jess was ready. She pulled her robe over her head and began to fasten a straight piece of branch around her middle. Then with a grimace, took Kat's bad hand, and put her other hand on her elbow, then pulled gently. The broken bone slipped under her torn skin. The pain wasn't as bad this time. Jess helped her back into her robe, carefully guiding it over her broken body.

"How's that? Can you walk? Is it working?" Jess' words came fast.

Kat took a few steps and found herself to be pretty stable. At least stable enough to fake it.

"I think it does," Kat said.

"What about the pain? I know you were trying to hide it last time, but it obviously hurt."

"It hurts a little bit. But not as bad. I can deal with it."

"Perfect. Now let's see what we can do about that face," Jess said.

Kat sat down and Jess began to work.

10

Jess held up a mirror to Kat's face when she had finished. She hadn't used the paint from her canvas paintings, but a kind of watercolor palette. Kat didn't remember make-up being a thing in heaven because you could just wish it onto your face. Using art supplies made for a perfect clandestine improvisational make-up. She looked at her face and was amazed. The contouring she had done around her nose and cheeks made her look entirely different. She looked as if she was barely wearing make up at all. Just a little mascara and light lipstick. It was almost magic.

"Wow," Kat said. "Just wow."

Jess beamed proudly, then pulled a pair of scissors from her glittery robe pocket.

"Just one more thing," she said. "Full disclosure though, I was not a hairdresser."

Jess pulled the front of Kat's hair in front of her face, leveled the scissors to her eyebrows and cut straight across. Then went around the rest of her hair and cut it to just above her shoulders. A bob with bangs. Simple, but effective. Kat looked nothing like Kat. Jess held up the mirror once again.

Kat looked into it and sighed, "Thanks. I hate it."

Jess smiled, "Ok, what now?"

Kat handed the mirror back to her, "I'd like to find my dad. I think he is the best person to help us gather the people who want to leave. I can trust him."

"Do you remember where he lives? I couldn't get a lot of information, but I'm pretty sure a lot has changed since you left."

"I think I do. Follow me."

Jess followed Kat through the fruit trees and into the main part of heaven. Kat made a mental note to collect some for her demon man. The ground felt soft and warm on her bare feet. Even the cobblestones felt like a massage. Still, she longed for her worn-in converse. Her robe was itchy as hell, like it didn't want to be on her as much as she didn't want to wear it. They walked past the park where Jesus' preferred platform stood. She was happy he wasn't there spouting his weird nonsense. There were a few angels mulling about, she smiled as she remembered her and Lucifer's glutinous display. One of the few memories she had of having fun in Heaven. None of the angels looked in her direction. It occurred to her that she hadn't seen any angels with wings this time around. They appeared to be gossiping or maybe she just assumed they were. She tried not to look like she was expecting to be called out at any moment. To just walk naturally, like she was supposed to be there.

"You look like a shoplifter who is trying not to look like a shoplifter," Jess said quietly to her.

Kat tried again to not look suspicious. As they got closer to the angels, two females and one male, all blonde, she could hear them talking softly. But not what they were saying. They looked over and sneered.

"Oh Hi!" Jess called and waved to them. They all looked over, dropped their sneers, and waved, before going back to their whispered conversation.

"They don't seem to have changed much," Kat said under her breath.

"Yeah, it reminds me of a middle school cafeteria," Jess replied, matching Kat's volume.

"Or the strip club dressing room, except at least strippers have each other's backs when it really counts. These fucking angels wouldn't piss on you if you were on fire. They'd smile and ask you how it felt."

"I mean, they can't piss, so?" Jess said and they both started laughing. "Are all the angels previously human?"

"I think most of them, but some are like Satan's minions or my dude Amon. Never human. I've never seen a child angel; I suspect that would be bad for God's image. A reminder that dying kids are all apart of His mysterious ways is probably not a good look. But I did find out when I was here, that I could steal some of the halos. Without the halos, genitals come back. It improved the angel's disposition considerably. Started an orgy in fact."

Jess reached up and started to yank on her halo. It wouldn't budge.

"What the fuck?" Jess said, not bothering to keep her voice down.

"Yeah, I think God fixed that when He found out. The dick. It doesn't seem like wings are an option anymore either."

They walked past the Administration building and Kat thought briefly about going in and getting set up, as if she were newly dead. But then thought better of it. So far it was going well, and they had passed about a dozen of Heaven's inhabitants without any hint of recognition. So far so good, she didn't want to push her luck. God seemed to only perpetuate the illusion of knowing everything, Kat didn't think He actually did. Just what exactly He knew or could know was still a mystery. Of course, His brand was supposed to be all knowing and all good. Kat was positive He wasn't the latter or the former.

As they walked past the bright shiny building, Kat began to recognize the street where her house had been. She turned to walk down it and toward her house, which she didn't expect to be there any longer. And soon she saw she was right. The house numbers stayed the same, but all the houses looked different. The house next door to hers which belonged to the cannibal serial killer, was now a cute white and yellow one. A dark-haired lady was sitting on a porch swing, humming to herself.

"That's where that killer dude lived," Kat pointed to the now not so grim looking little home. "And that was mine," she pointed to the now light green home next to it. It had a well-kept lawn, which wasn't saying much, as all the lawns were well kept, and looked to be occupied, but Kat couldn't see by whom.

"That doesn't look like a killer's house," she said. "What did it look like before?"

"It was plain and brown, and once I saw the guy come out with blood on his mouth," Kat replied. She looked at the house on the other side of her used-to-be heaven house to where her other neighbor had lived. Once again, the numbers were the same, but the house was totally different. Kat pointed to it, "A lady lived there, she said she had killed her kids and husband. It looks different now."

"Wow, that's pretty fucked up Kat."

"Dude, I know. She got all mad about it when I was like 'Wow that's pretty fucked up'. Called me a slut and said I had been forgiven too, as if that is somehow worse than killing kids." Kat rolled her eyes.

Kat saw the street where her father had lived and directed Jess toward it. She was relieved to see that it hadn't changed. She opened the gate and they both stepped through, Kat knocked on the door and closed her eyes as she waited for an answer. The door opened in a second and her eyes shot open. Her father stood there. His eyes were as wide as hers. Beelzebub, his dog sat wagging his tail behind him. He stared at her curiously for a moment, but then despite the makeover, he seemed to recognize her.

"Kathryn?" He said. "Oh my God, is that you?" He looked to be drunk, hammered in fact, at first, but sobered up as he spoke. In Hell, you had to wait for your buzz to wear off, but in Heaven, you could just wish your buzz gone. It was how they kept the booze flowing for eternity.

"It is," Kat through her arms around him. He hugged her tightly.

"Come in. Right now," he said and ushered them both inside, before slamming the door shut behind them. He closed the blinds on the front window. "How did you get back, I heard you were sent to Hell. Are you ok?"

"I'm fine, perfect in fact." She checked to make sure her sleeve was still hiding her broken arm, "This is Jess. Jess this is my dad, Dave."

Jess held out her hand and he took it in a soft handshake. "Nice to meet you."

"You look so different," he said to Kat. "Were you really in Hell?"

"This is just temporary while I visit here. I was dad, and still am kind of. Or at least I'm going back."

"Why?" He looked concerned.

Kat had taken a seat on her dad's little sofa, while Jess had sat down in the recliner across from it. A small perfect little coffee table completed the furnishings in the little living room. On it sat a bottle of one hundred proof Ever clear liquor. *Wine is fine, but Whisky's quicker, and Ever Clear will fuck you up in an instant,* Kat thought with dismay. He seemed to have upped his getting fucked up forever game.

"Heaven is a lie, Dad." She had told him this before she left, but his memory seemed to be distorted.

He looked down at his lap and hung a hand over the side of the sofa to pat Beelzebub between the ears. "God is good," he whispered.

"Yeah, about that. Dad, I know you must have figured this out. What did you hear after I left?"

He looked around as if someone were listening, then spoke in a whisper, "I heard that you had caused some trouble and were sent to Hell. They said some awful things about you Kathryn." She cringed at that, knowing it was probably the slut thing. "Then nothing, no one talked about it anymore. And then some things changed."

"Like what?" Kat asked, Jess listened intently, but with her eyes on the bottle.

"Well, some of the…well…angels have been moved. The repentant have their own space now. A lot less mixing."

"That makes sense. My neighbors were both self-righteous murderers, and that was my first clue."

"I don't think we should be talking like this, Kat," he looked around again. "God sees everything."

"He doesn't though. How do you think I caused all that trouble?"

Jess looked at him and shrugged. Her dad thought for a moment and shrugged back. "Ok, but He's still God. You mean to tell me that Hell is really better than Heaven?"

"Exactly dad. Please trust me when I say that this is all a façade. God is a di… jerk. He doesn't care about what people do or how they might hurt other people on earth, He only cares about being worshipped. I met Him. Spoke to Him."

Her dad closed his eyes for a moment, "I know you're right Kat. But we're talking about God here. Like God."

"Right. But what do we really know about Him? Just what we learned on earth and after we died. He controls a lot, but He is not the all-powerful all-good being He pretends to be. This is going to sound weird, but Satan is the good guy in this scenario. There is real freedom in Hell. It's not all flowers and sausages, but it's honest. It's just. Bad people aren't rewarded. People are good to each other for real. Not just for show." She thought about adding the sex thing but decided against it. She didn't want to know if her dad was into orgies or not.

"I believe you Kathryn. I guess I knew all this before," he glanced at the half full bottle on the table, that would never be empty. "I know, or I think a lot of people saw that after you left. Then it was all brushed under the rug. I'm not the only one now that knows or suspects the truth. They just wish they didn't."

"Will you help me? I want to bring them to Hell," Kat said.

"I will, but how?"

Jess broke her silence, "So I have a plan." Kat really liked this chick. "We need to contact as many people as possible and let them know. Spread the gospel of Hell if you will. And who better to spread the gospel than Jesus." Jess beamed a dazzling smile.

Kat and her dad just stared at her.

"Hear me out. Jesus is a void. He was only ever just a pawn in God's twisted ass game. Have you ever actually talked to him? He's empty, there's not much going on there. My guess is that it's a bad idea to breed a human with a deity. Let's get him to do it. People will listen."

"Don't you think God will notice His kid switched sides?" Kat asked.

"According to you, God gives no fucks about anything but Himself."

Kat had to admit she had her there, "True. But how do you we get him to do that?" If Kat had been on earth, she knew exactly how she would do it. She gave one hell of a lap dance, a dude with blue balls would do just about anything. She had even danced for a guy in a Jesus costume once. But the real Jesus in Heaven was probably missing his dick, unlike her customer in the plastic crown of thorns.

"We feed him some new scripture. We get him to preach it. We don't need to him to say Satan is good and Hell is paradise. It's not like any of the bible is clear cut. Just some vague stuff that can be interpreted that way, we plant the seeds and hope they grow the vines that lead people to follow us to Hell."

"That is fucking brilliant, beat the fucker at his own game," Dave said. Kat cringed at the f-bombs. She had been a little kid when he died and had never heard him curse.

"Dude, I think that could work," Kat said. She got up off the couch and planted a wet kiss squarely on her new friend's mouth. She lingered just a little longer than she had intended, and discovered she liked it.

11

"I'm done with this stuff," Kat's father said, as he knocked the bottle of liquor from his coffee table. It didn't have a chance to soak into the rug before it was gone. Messes aren't a thing in Heaven. No broken glass or stains either. Beelzebub looked up at him from the side of the sofa and licked his hand. He seemed to be happy with his person's declaration. "Enough of this bull-pucky." Kat liked his mock swearing much better than his F-bombs.

"Good for you dad," Kat said, as she stood up.

He walked with Jess and Kat to the front door and gave Kat a long hug as they said goodbye. Kat told him they would be back after they sorted out more of the details. They walked down his path and to the road toward Jess' house. The cobblestone street shimmered in the bright sunlight of Heaven as they walked. Kat thought about asking Jess about her life on earth but decided against it. Her memories were probably murky already, and she thought it might be frustrating too for her to try and remember what Heaven wanted her to forget. Kat had struggled with the memory of her mother when she had first died. Heaven, God, and Jesus had done nothing to help. Jess didn't seem like she wanted to talk about her life anyway but was totally enthralled by Kat's stories of her exploits in Heaven before she escaped.

When they reached Jess' little Heaven house, not far from her father's, Kat giggled at the eclectic abode. It was electric blue, with a smattering of flowers in the front yard. Not much rhyme or reason to it but still had a sense of order somehow. There could have been a rhyme or reason for it, just one that wasn't obvious to Kat. The colors both didn't mesh and perfectly meshed all at the same time. The entire vibe of the place was of a kind of calm chaos. Kat didn't believe much in fate or luck, but that this was the person she had first contact with seemed like it had been divine intervention. It felt meant to be. Although exactly who meant what, Kat didn't know.

Jess opened the unlocked door. Unlocked because locks didn't exist in Heaven. The inside of her home matched the outside. It was warm and inviting, and if Kat thought if it lacked anything, it was a cat.

"Would you like some tea or something?" Jess asked.

"I would love a fucking donut," she said. She had wanted to resist this vulgar temptation of Heaven, but the request was out of her mouth before she had a chance to realize that she had asked for it. "And a cup of tea." Normally, she wouldn't have asked for anything, lest it put the host out. But in Heaven all one has to do is wish. Ask and you shall receive. Unless of course God, doesn't want you to have it. Like weed. Or genitals.

Kat took a seat at the small kitchen table opposite Jess. A cup of tea appeared along with a sprinkled donut. Kat eyed the pastry suspiciously and decided she would let it sit there. Hoping it would get stale but knowing it wouldn't. Thirty seconds later, she took a huge bite.

"Stupid perfect donut," Kat said as sprinkles rained down onto the table. They disappeared the moment they hit.

"What?" Jess asked.

"You'll understand when you get to Hell."

Jess shrugged and took a sip of her own tea. "Ok, so I was thinking we write our own chapter of the bible. Or a verse or whatever."

"I'm listening," Kat said. Listening was about all she could do with her mouth full of donut.

"But we have to *write it,* write it, no wishing." A typewriter appeared on the table in front of her and she began to type. "We know that God doesn't see everything as He wants everyone to think, I think it's better if we keep the wishing or manifesting to a minimum."

"It needs to be vague, but not too vague." Kat said, thinking that was an utterly unhelpful suggestion, but not knowing what else to say.

"Can't say I read much of the bible on earth," Jess said.

Her fingers were a blur on the keyboard. The typewriter wasn't the old timey kind with individual metal buttons, but one that looked almost like a laptop she had remembered on earth. There would be no internet connection because there was no internet. There would be no need for a printer either, for as she typed, a paper with her printed words spooled out of the top. Kat took the paper as she finished and read it over, she smiled when she was done.

"I think this could work," Kat said.

"We just need to find the guy and get him to read it."

"Do you think it will be that easy?"

"I do," Jess said. "I tried to talk to him when I first got here. Didn't know much about him, but I figured, since he was supposed to have died so I could get to heaven, I owed it to him to get to know him a little."

"I guess maybe I should have done that," Kat said.

"Oh, no. You shouldn't have. Like I said, there's not much there. He's like an empty record player. A player piano with no keys. There's no substance. He speaks in riddles he doesn't even understand. I think that's by design. Everything he says resonates with someone because he doesn't really say anything at all. People simply hear what they want to hear. They interpret things as they want them to be. There's no real message. Other than to love God or else."

"No one, not even God will be expecting Jesus to be touting the benefits of Hell. Now to find him."

"He comes to the platform every day to preach. Let's just wait there," Jess said, standing up from her seat.

"Sweet, let's go," Kat said, but as she tried to stand up, another donut appeared. Kat meant to leave it on the table, but it was in her hand as they walked out the door. *Stupid perfect donut,* she thought as they stepped out into the perfect day. She left a trail of sprinkles in her wake.

The platform where Jesus preached was a little farther away, but Jess' legs didn't tire despite the distance. Although, if Kat missed a step, her back felt a little wobbly, and her legs were starting to get tired. Kat looked into the sky and saw nothing but blue. Somewhere in Heaven lurked the worst of the worst. People who should be in Hell, amusing the demons with their screams and bloodied heads. Instead, they were enjoying their cruel delights as a reward for their servitude and worship. Just now, they were kept much more on the down low. Because of her, she assumed. She smiled at what a huge pain the non-existent ass she had been.

They found Jesus standing next to his platform and not on it. He was chewing on a piece of Heaven fruit, and despite the juice dripping onto his beard, it made Kat's mouth water. She remembered the mealy apple she'd had while Bobby the hairdressing demon processed her hair. She didn't want to admit that Heaven had its charms, but it did. She found herself breaking for one of the trees that held the special fruit Jesus was eating, before she realized what she was doing. She plucked a piece and took a bite. She closed her eyes as the juice flooded her mouth. When she opened them again, she saw that Jesus was up on the stage with Jess' prose in his hands. She looked down at the half-eaten fruit in her and dropped it on the ground. She brought her bare foot down onto it and mashed it into the dirt. She steeled herself for the unpleasant sensation of the soft, squishy, and wet fruit spurting between her toes, but it didn't come. Instead, the fruit enveloped her foot like the hand of a talented masseuse. What should have been revolting, was instead warm and soothing. She frowned at her foot and walked to where Jess was standing close to the platform, pausing to wipe her foot clean on the grass.

"I think he's waiting for people to come," Jess said in a low voice. "I told him it was a new verse from his dad. He didn't ask any questions, just thanked me and took the paper."

Kat realized she had missed this exchange while she was distracted. Angels of all kinds had started to walk up and surround the platform. Jess was looking at her a little strangely, and she wondered just how long she had been standing by the fruit tree.

"Sorry, I checked out there for a second," she asked Jess. "Not sure what was going on there."

"You did. But I just figured you really wanted to have some fruit before you went back to Hell.

Kat was about to tell her that she hadn't really intended to go to the tree, but before she could Jesus began to speak.

"Behold! The greatness of Heaven and all its fruits. We are lost but found, full but empty, enlightened but in search of mystery. We are all God's children in death and life. He grants us peace in return for our conformity. Our utter devotion fuels his soul, as He grants precious salvation to the wretched. He finds comfort in the retribution of those He sends to Hell for their sin of life," Jesus raised his arms as he spoke. "For our fear of Him, He grants us whatever He wishes us to have. As no one knows better what we want or who we should be. He tells us what makes us happy, thereby removing our burden of deciding for ourselves. This holy one, He loves us all, except for the ones He doesn't really care for. The old great one tells us He is perfect in His divine judgement. He loves us so much that He created this perfect place for those with blind faith, to live without sin, without our very humanity. Our souls live without the burden of earthly pleasures or the concern for others. For our only concern is Him." Jesus paused, with his eyes closed. Waiting for applause.

The crowd had grown mostly silent. Kat looked around at the angels staring at Jesus, some of them cocking their heads. Jesus opened one eye to the crowd, and when he saw that no applause was coming, consulted the paper in his hand and spoke louder.

"Behold! For God had created another realm for His creations. One of free will and fairness! One where all of your earthly body parts are restored. Where the cruel are punished and free will reigns. It is a realm that sacrifices the perfect for the genuine. The illusion for the truth, God has hidden this from His angels, so they will continue to worship Him in divine ignorance."

"I think it's working," Jess whispered.

Jesus stepped off the platform and started to walk toward the field where the portal to Hell was hidden. Jess and some of the angels followed him. Kat looked at the angels who chose to stay behind, wondering if she might recognize any of them. She didn't. They all looked new to her, but she figured that would make sense. There must be too many souls up here to count.

Kat heard Jesus talking as they walked. She had tried to pay attention to what he was saying but found she couldn't focus on his words. She found her mind drifting as she followed the group walking with Jesus. As they neared the clearing, she saw that some of the angels had peeled off and were no longer following. Kat closed her eyes as she walked, letting the sound of the others guide her feet. She found that she felt lovely, a sweet taste flooded her mouth, and the pain of her injuries had faded into oblivion.

A sudden jolt of pain shot up her arm, "Kat!" Jess said, with her hand gripping Kat's bad arm. "What the fuck are you doing?"

She opened her eyes to a scowling Jess, her face covered in orange goo.

"Uh, I don't know. I was just walking," Kat said. Her brain was kind of fuzzy.

"Yeah, you were. But then you stopped by that tree and started eating that fruit again. Then you spit it at me."

Kat didn't remember any of that.

"Sorry, but have you tried it. It's really good," Kat said lamely. She liked the fruit, but this was ridiculous.

"Just what got into my mouth when you spit it on me," Jess said. "And yeah, not a fan."

"Sorry, I don't know what happened," Kat said. She really didn't and it scared her.

Jesus and the dozen or so angels that had followed him, stopped just short of the portal. He had acquired a basket and was plucking fruit from a nearby tree. Kat didn't remember the tree being there when she came through. Soon, Jesus and the angels that had followed him were eating the fruit. They were only twenty feet from the entrance to the portal.

"Eat my friends, for God hates us all!" Jesus cried. The rest of the angels murmured in agreement. Orange muck coated their faces.

"What the actual fuck?" Kat said.

"I wish I knew. I don't get the thing with the fruit. I smelled it when I first got here, but it kind of turned me off," Jess said with bewilderment.

"You've never tried it?" Kat asked, remembering how wonderful it was. She found herself wanting another piece.

"No."

The crowd around Jesus, was starting to disperse.

"We got them this far, but I don't know how to get them down this hole to Hell. I don't think the message really stuck. And we want them to come down, not Jesus. Could you imagine the shitstorm if we accidently drug Jesus to Hell?" Kat giggled. "Not sure we thought this all the way through. I guess it was a little silly to think it would be that easy."

"I mean, so what? Aren't we trying to fuck with God?"

Kat smiled at her new friend, "I like the way you think, but maybe we want to wait until we get the souls that want to leave first. Then we can work on fucking with the big guy."

"Probably a good plan," Jess said.

They were standing on the edge of the boulders that hid the portal. Jesus and his followers had left the tree and were moving away. Kat didn't remember picking it, but she had stashed a piece of fruit in the pocket of her robe. She took it out, looked at it with disgust, and tossed it into the hole. She picked up a pebble and tossed it in after the fruit.

"I'm going to check in with Amon and see if he has any ideas about how to get them the rest of the way."

"Ooo… Heaven fruit," Kat heard Amon say from the dark hole behind the boulders. Kat was hoping that Amon was close enough that it wouldn't take him too long to come, but she hadn't expected him to arrive that quickly. "Uuuugggghhhhh……What the…" Amon didn't finish the fuck part. Kat heard retching sounds coming from the portal.

"Are you ok? No way it was rotten, that doesn't happen here," Kat said.

Amon didn't answer, just made more puking sounds. Kat stepped closer to the hole so she could see inside. She didn't want to enter it all the way in case she lost the make-up job she had. Inside a candle was burning near Amon. She could see him on the floor of the portal, licking up the dirt. He was moaning but seemed to have stopped puking.

"Dude, what are you doing?" She asked.

"Trust me, this tastes better," he said with a tongue full of dirt.

12

"That fucker," Kat said.

"What?" Jess asked.

"The fruit of ignorance. Jesus fucking Christ…"

"Wouldn't that just be Jesus jerking off?"

Kat raised an eyebrow at her but started laughing anyway.

Amon was close to the entrance now, but not close enough to take his demon form in Heaven. Kat was glad he was worried about that, he was hideous, and she didn't think it would be a great idea for Jess to see him that way. She told him how she had kind of blanked out when she ate the fruit this time.

"It seems that God has figured out how to keep them all complacent through that fruit. Keep them dumb. He's a dick, but not a stupid one," Kat said. "That must be why I kept zoning out."

"That sounds about right," Satan said, scaring the holy shit out of all of them. Jess backed a little further away from the entrance. "Given His first stupid magic trick was the fruit of knowledge, this makes sense."

"He didn't want Adam and Eve to eat that fruit…" Jess said.

"Bullshit. Why else would He put it there? And create a Hell to put people in because Eve ate it? He definitely wanted people to eat it. How else would such a dick like that get people to like Him? Coercion and extortion. He needed leverage of some kind," Satan said. "And you must be Jess. I've heard awesome things about you. Great job you did with Kat there. I barely recognized her. She looks like she belongs there," He paused. "Except she is missing her halo."

Kat reached up over her head with her good arm, "Fuck."

"Oops. Totally forgot. No one seemed to notice though," Jess said. "And nice to meet you." Kat couldn't tell if Jess really thought it was nice to meet him or if she was just being nice. She made a note to tell her about the orgy head dicks later. Kat hoped Jess was into orgies, as that seemed like a pretty good ice breaker when hanging out with the ruler of Hell.

"Probably because of the fruit," Kat said. "But it is also making it so our message isn't going to stick."

"On the bright side, you still have your pussy," Amon said.

"Not that it will be any use in a realm where there are no dicks," Kat rolled her eyes at him, then turned to Satan. "So, what do we do about the fruit? And my halo?"

"The halo I can fix right now," a golden ring appeared in Satan's hand enormous hand. Kat reached into the hole and took it from him. Taking a moment to admire his fingers. She burned the image of them in her mind, in the hope that she could use the memory as a counter to the heaven donut's vile temptation. The next time she thought about eating one of the stupid things, she would remember the big red guy's talented fingers. Kat held the halo over her head and let go. It landed with a thud and bounced away.

"Oww," she said rubbing the top of her head.

"Oops, sorry. Here let me try again."

Satan produced another golden ring but blew on it this time before he handed it to Kat through the portal. Kat took it, and once again placed it over her head, but before she let it go, she said to him, "You're not fucking with me, are you?"

Satan put a huge finger to his forehead, his chest, then each breast right to left, making the sign of the cross, before holding up two fingers in a peace sign, "Scouts honor."

Kat let go and the halo floated above her head. She lifted her robe to check to see if her lady bits were still there. And gave a thumbs up when she saw that they were.

"I make way better halos," Satan beamed.

"It doesn't reflect the sunlight," Jess said, noticing the lack of sparkle on the hell halo. "But I doubt anyone will notice."

"That's settled, now what do we do about the damned fruit?" Kat asked.

"What if we had our own fruit of knowledge?" Amon said.

"Like plant trees or something? And honestly, I'm not sure how we would compete with this fruit now. It's kind of hard to resist," Kat said.

Satan and Amon sat just inside the portal, while Kat and Jess sat just outside. While they were pondering what to do Jess produced a cup of tea and sipped thoughtfully. Then she produced a sprinkled donut like the one Kat had in her kitchen only a short time before. Kat looked at it with lust in her eyes.

"Would you like one?" Jess held it to her mouth and licked off a few sprinkles. Satan winked at her, and a slight crease in her brow appeared.

"Ugh, I'm trying to resist, but fuck it. Okay," Kat said, forgetting to remember Satan's fat fingers. One appeared in her hand. She was just about to bite into it and said, "Dude." Kat took a bite, and said around a mouthful of pastry, "What about donuts?"

Amon cocked his head, "How would that work?"

But Satan was tracking, "Satan's donuts of knowledge. I can dig it." He produced a sprinkled donut much like the one

Kat was holding, but it was blood red, with black frosting. Kat threw hers to the ground and took the one Satan had offered. She took a bite.

"Uh… it's good…" She didn't want to finish it, the damned thing was a little stale.

"You're a creature from Hell. Let me try," Jess snatched the donut out of her hand and stuffed it in her mouth. "Nope this is fucking delicious. Omg…"

"Oh my Lemmy is what we say in Hell," Amon informed her.

"Lemmy?"

"Lemmy Kilmister the Patron saint of Rock and Roll *and* Daisy Dukes?" Amon rolled his eyes, and Kat gave him a dirty look. She was kind of hoping that her new friend and her boyfriend would get along in hell.

"Oh, my bad," she said rolling her eyes back at him. And Kat knew then that they would get along just fine.

"So do you think this could work?" Kat asked Satan.

"Maybe, like I said, a lot of what goes on in Heaven and its rules aren't known to me. But I can get you all the enchanted donuts you need. You just have to figure out how to get them to the people, and they can decide for themselves where they would rather be without God's interference."

"There's always the door-to-door thing," Kat said.

"Not something I've ever advocated for," said Satan sternly. Not so stern as to be scary, but he was Satan so still pretty scary.

"Yeah, but how many missionaries bring donuts?" Kat offered.

"True," Satan scratched his big ugly chin.

"What if the fruit counteracts the donuts though?" Amon said.

"What if we sabotage the fruit?" Kat said. She had picked up her Heaven donut from the ground and started eating it again. She wasn't sure if the five second rule applied in Heaven but figured Heaven dirt couldn't hurt.

"I don't know that I could get behind poisoning people," Jess added. "Although, I guess they're dead already. We don't want to make them sick though.

"Nah, we could just make it taste like ass," Kat said.

"I kind of like the taste of ass," Satan said. Kat knew he spoke the truth. She had seen him lick plenty at the orgy. Satan was a giver. "But I get it, what you mean. How about the birds?"

"The birds?" Jess said.

"Well, Kat was able to give her Heaven cat a butthole. What if we fed the birds some special seed, they get buttholes, and poop on the fruit?" Satan was having fun now. "Won't hurt anybody, just taste like shit."

"Dude, evil," Jess smiled.

"Kind of my jam," Satan winked again at her, but less lewdly. Jess winked back this time. *Perfect,* Kat thought, *friends if not lovers.*

Satan clapped his hands, and immediately a rumbling could be heard from the bowels of the portal. Two minions appeared behind him.

"Joey, get me a fuck ton of bird seed please. And Parker, ask Julia to whip us up a fuck ton of these donuts," Satan produced another black and red donut.

Jess frowned, "Uh… Satan? Maybe black and red aren't the most low-key colors for Heaven?"

"Ahhh… good catch my love. Tell her to make them golden with sparkly icing."

Joey and Parker bowed and disappeared into the dark portal.

Jess getting bolder with the Lord of Darkness said, "That's perfect. But I have a question. If you can just make stuff appear, why do you need minions to go get them?"

Satan smiled, "Because not all of my minions enjoy the violence and gore of the punishment assignments."

"Just the really baddies get punished," Kat interjected.

"Yes, just the baddies," Satan agreed. "But I don't want to destroy them or make them do things that they find upsetting. Some of them are quite sensitive creatures. So, I give them other jobs to do. Jobs they find fulfilling and enjoy. They aren't like humans, more like pets or dogs on earth. They like to help. For some of them, it's playing with severed heads, or stripping the skin off of people who forget to return their library books. But others need less bloody tasks."

"People who forget to return their library books?" Jess frowned.

"He's kidding," Kat said as Satan flashed a hideously goofy smile.

Jess frowned again, "Sorry to ask so many questions, but I have another one."

"Shoot, my love. I'll answer what I can."

"Won't God notice His birds have started shitting and that there are new donuts in Heaven?"

"He didn't know about the weed, until someone told Him. And so far, hasn't noticed the new portal. Or Kat and her missing halo, for that matter. I think He'll figure it out at some point. But hopefully we can reach as many souls as we can before He does. He won't admit it, but He doesn't know everything. He can't. No one can. Deity or not. He has just done a great job of making people believe that. We're essentially banking on His own arrogance."

"It does seem like there's a lot to bank on. How long until…" Jess began but was interrupted by the sound of a minion bounding down the portal.

"Ah… Joey! Good job!" Satan patted his minion on the head, the minion cooed. He had been pushing a wheelbarrow full of small sacks. Satan dismissed the demon and pushed the wheelbarrow toward the entrance to Heaven. He waved his large hand over the top of it. "Your bird seed, my lady," he said to Kat and bowed.

Amon began chucking the sacks into Heaven. Jess picked up one of the small canvas sacks and pulled the string at the top. She walked toward the nearest tree and made kissy noises to the birds as she spilled the seed on the ground. A little yellow Heaven bird hopped down and began to peck at the seed. It opened and shut its beak a few times then stopped cold. Jess looked concerned, then pissed. "You said we wouldn't hurt anyone."

"I would never hurt an animal," Satan sounded offended. "Just wait."

Jess turned back to the little bird, which suddenly hopped up in the air and expelled a small white squirt of heavenly bird poop. Then it pecked at more seed. Its buddies in the tree had been watching the whole affair and soon there were a dozen or more birds pecking at the ground. They began to chirp at each other happily, as Jess tossed more seed on the ground.

"There see?" Satan lowered his eyes at her, "I'm not a dick."

"Sorry."

"No worries. The donuts will take a little more time. Come back tomorrow, and in the meantime go forth and spread my seed!"

Satan bowed laughing at his cum joke and turned to down the portal. Kat met Amon at the thin line between Heaven and the portal to Hell. He leaned in so that just his lips were in the light, they became red and lined with course fur, but Kat kissed them anyway.

"Be careful Kat. I want you back in Hell." He hiccupped and produced a flame that singed her face. It hurt, but Kat didn't care. "I'll be back to check on you tomorrow."

Kat picked up a few of the sacks and stowed them in the pockets of her robe. She took the rest of them and hid them behind some of the boulders near the entrance. She and Jess walked toward Jess' house spreading bird seed under every tree they passed along the way. Birds in Heaven had been lively so much as Kat remembered. Frolicking about with the squirrels. After they ate however, they frolicked, but with a bit more gusto. Not quite like her cat Lucifer, who could talk, and was far too proud of his new ass for her tastes. But it was funny to watch them discover food and what happens after. She had wondered if it was just wishful thinking that the fruit would end up covered in bird poop. But as cats on earth liked to present their buttholes to anyone willing or not, birds in heaven happily shat on everything.

"Well, they seem happy," Jess said.

Kat smiled at her, "It is funny how we miss the things we find inconvenient on earth, when we learn that they don't exist in Heaven."

They came upon Jesus' platform, it was empty. There were a few angels milling about. Some smelling flowers or talking amongst themselves. Kat had to admit that for the most part, they seemed happy. She wondered again if this was the right thing to do. To try and enlighten the people in Heaven. Who was she to say whether they were happy here or not.

A dark-haired female angel moved toward a group of other angels, who didn't seem to notice her approach. She had eyes slightly too big for her face and an unfortunate overbite, Kat didn't think she was ugly by any standard, plain maybe. She was smiling as she approached them. But when one of the angels saw that she was coming toward them, a tall redheaded angel with stunning blue eyes and large breasts, straining the front of her sparkly robe, the smile bled from her face. The redhead smirked at her and alerted the other two angels in her group. They all turned to her with looks of disgust and began to walk away. The dark-haired angel's shoulders drooped toward the ground, and she turned to walk in the other direction. Kat couldn't know where but wouldn't have been surprised to learn that the angel was heading back to her lonely little house to drink herself stupid. Kat wanted to run and kick the redheaded angel squarely in the pussy, or maybe another extra sensitive part. But she only looked to

Jess, who wore a face almost as sad as the poor rejected bug eyed angel.

Neither Kat nor Jess saw or heard Jesus as he snuck up behind them.

"Hello, my little lambs," he said.

"Uh, hello," Kat said, hoping the exchange would be brief. She had a really bad habit of picking fights with heavenly deities. Thankfully, Jess intervened.

"Hello Jesus," she said and dazzled him with a warm smile, he smiled back.

A small flock of birds took off from a nearby tree and Kat and Jess watched with horror as a white glob landed in the middle of the son of God's forehead. His smile stuck as his eyes crossed and looked upward, as if he would be able to see what had just hit him in the face. Kat thought this would have made a much better portrait than the one that her mother had hung in the dining room. Jess turned to see that her friend was giving her an *oh fuck* look. Kat thought for sure this would be it.

Jesus reached up and wiped away the bird poo, smile intact and, "Would either of you ladies be interested in washing my feet?"

"Uh, I'm good," Kat said, and wondered why she couldn't just keep her mouth shut.

"Ok. Have a blessed evening," Jesus said and walked away.

13

"Let's go find that angel," Jess said, already trotting in the direction that the snubbed and not quite ugly angel had gone in. Kat knew she wasn't asking so much as telling her that's what they were doing. She tried to run but found that the patch job on her spine wouldn't allow her to keep up.

"Hang on. I'm all smoke and mirrors here, not quite intact. I have to walk."

Jess slowed down, stopped and waited, "Ok, but I don't want to lose her. We might not find her again."

When Kat reached her, she had to stop and catch her breath. Jess jittered her legs, obviously anxious to keep moving. Kat adjusted the brace under her robe, and they began to fast walk, sprinkling bird seed along the way. It wasn't long before they saw the angel they were looking for. She had turned down a deserted street full of little pastel and white painted gingerbread Heaven houses. This road looked as if it were governed by a stringent HOA. Every house lacked the brilliant chaos of Jess'. Other than different colors, all the houses looked much the same.

"Hey!" Jess called to the angel. She turned around and eyed them suspiciously. Kat grabbed her bad arm to make sure the sleeve hadn't rolled up to show her gruesome injury. The bone may have slid back in place, but the wound was still there, unpleasant to look at. The sight of it would make it obvious that there was something off about her.

"Hey," the angel called back tentatively, but kept walking.

"We want to talk to you," Jess said. "We want to be your friend."

The angel walked faster and opened one of the white picket fence gates. Kat cringed. This angel had been rejected too many times to believe that anyone wanted to be her friend. Kat got it.

"We just want to talk for a few, those angels were shitty. I know. They were to me too," Kat called loudly. She hoped to Lemmy that no one heard her on this quiet little street. The angel stopped at her front door and turned to look at them.

"Ok, stay there, please. I'll come to you," the angel said. She walked back to her gate where Kat and Jess stood. She didn't open it.

Jess opened her mouth to say something, but Kat thought she would be better for this initial exchange. She figured Jess would forgive her interruption.

"I saw those angels being dicks to you. I had that happen too. I get it, I promise. This isn't the easiest place to make friends. I'm Kat, and this is Jess. Jess put up her hand but took Kat's cue and stayed quiet.

"I'm Alice," the angel said, but not warmly. "I don't like to call people…uh angels, names. They weren't so bad."

Bullshit, Kat thought.

"They can't hear you," Kat said. "Did they tell you they could?"

Alice looked down at her feet and said in a low voice, "The angel at the admin office said all negative comments about the favorite angels would be heard."

Kat twisted to look around, "Hey fuck wads!" She yelled as loud as could. "Do you hear me calling you fuck wads? You dicks hear me?"

Alice and Jess cringed in tandem but relaxed when no one came to smite them.

"See? Nothing. They just said that, 'cause they're dicks. I promise," Kat said.

Neither Alice nor Jess looked convinced.

"Can we come inside and talk?" Jess said. "We're not ax murderers," Jess flashed that dazzling smile again, but it slithered away when Alice recoiled. "Sorry, bad joke."

"I'm guessing you've run across a redeemed ax murderer or two in Heaven, right? I get that too," Kat said.

"No, not an ax murderer per se. This lady strangled people and beat people to death and slit someone's throat. She killed a couple of guys with an ax, but swore it was self-defense. I think she even poisoned someone. Multitalented she was. But that was before she found Jesus," she rolled her eyes. "Ok, come in."

She opened her gate to allow them to follow her to her lavender colored front door. The sunlight glittered off the white trim. They walked into the little house. Inside was painted pale yellow, no pictures hung on the walls, and it was sparsely furnished. Only a small white sofa and tiny coffee table graced the tiny living room. It looked just like all the other houses, hers included. She had no TV or stereo. Where one would be stood a large bookcase filled with books. Kat scanned the titles.

"Some of them are blank inside," Alice said sadly. "But some have just been censored. The sex scenes or anything else that I guess isn't acceptable here."

"Oh wow," Kat said. She had pulled a copy of Salman Rushdie's Satanic Verses and flipped it open to find the pages entirely blank. "This wasn't even about the same religion, why would they ban it?"

"Different religion, same god," Alice said.

Kat shrugged.

"The curse words have all been replaced with 'dang' and 'fudge'," Jess said. She was holding a copy of Stephen King's The Stand. "Jeez…the Bible must be blank too. It's full of sex and violence."

"I'd be surprised if anyone here read the Bible. Certainly not if they were Catholic," Kat laughed. Thinking this must be God's version of that fucked up episode of the Twight Zone. An endless amount of time to read, but only what He approved of.

"Might as well all be blank. Please sit. You look tired…" Alice said. Looking at Kat, the suspicion in her eyes returned. Kat thought she needed to get her job done and get the fuck back to Hell.

"There's a reason for why I look kind of…weird," Kat said.

"How long have you been here?" Jess said, in an attempt to dismantle the awkwardness that Kat had created.

"I don't know. You guys want a drink? I didn't drink at all when I was alive. But now, it's the only thing that passes the time."

Kat and Jess both shook their heads.

"Listen, I'm just going to come right out with it. So, I was here, and then… well, and then I left." Kat said.

"Left?"

"And went to Hell," Kat cringed. "Ok, I know it sounds bad, but Satan has these really cool penises on his head sometimes. And his fingers. Holy fuckballs. They're magic."

"What she means is, when Kat came here, the angels were real assholes to her. Like they are. She ended up like you. Trying to drink away eternity. But she discovered that this whole place is one big lie," Jess said, her words flew like bullets out of her mouth.

"No offense, but it's not that much of a stretch to see that this place isn't quite like it's sold on the brochure. Honestly,

I think most people are here because the alternative is much worse," Alice said.

"That's what we're trying to tell you. I went to Hell, and it's awesome," Kat said. "Ok, so not totally awesome. More like mediocre awesome. You get zits and stuff. You can't wish for anything, but I promise there's not a book there with 'fudge' instead of 'fuck'. In fact, there's lots of fucking. If you're into it of course. Consent and respecting boundaries are mandatory."

"You know… I completely believe you. I've thought that this place stinks. But most of the time when I start to have thoughts like that, they kind of go away. Like they're hard to hold on to."

"Do you like the Heaven fruit," Jess asked, and Alice cocked her head.

"Yes, but what does that matter?"

"It makes you stupid," Kat said.

"No, not stupid." Jess looked at her sideways, "But it does influence your thoughts about Heaven and God. It kind of erases critical thinking. So not, stupid, but ignorant."

"Really?" Alice said, "That explains so much."

"Right? It didn't do that when I was here. I think God made it that way after I escaped. Pretty sure that's why you were told that the angels could hear your shit talking too."

"I don't even need to hear anymore. I want to get the fuck out of here," Alice stood up.

"We can totally help you, but we want to reach more people," Jess held up her almost empty sack with bird seed in it. "Satan's seed," she beamed, but then she saw Alice cringe. "Bird seed. It makes the birds poop, and their poop renders the fruit disgusting."

Alice sat down again, "That's way better than what I was thinking."

"Tomorrow, we're going to get special donuts that will counteract the effects of the fruit. Satan's donuts of knowledge," Kat tried to mimic Jess' smile but felt the paint on her face crack.

"Ha! Donuts of knowledge," Alice smiled. She was beautiful when she smiled.

"We've written a verse and given it to Jesus, he's already preaching it. And once we distribute the donuts, we're going to try and lead the people who want to come out of here."

"Ah… Jesus, not too bright that one." Alice frowned and looked around her living room as if it might be bugged.

"Come on. We'll show you the portal and you can help us spread the seed. If you want to that is," Kat said.

"Hell yeah!" Alice giggled.

They stood up and Jess held up a hand to high five Alice, they smacked hands. Then Alice turned to Kat and held up her hand, Kat high fived her as well. But it didn't go as smoothly as when Jess did it. She forgot to use her good arm, and the force of the smack popped her bone back out and her forearm bent backward. Blood began to seep from the rip in her skin. Skin that still had glitter stubbornly sticking to it.

Alice gasped. So did Kat, but not because she was surprised or horrified, but because it hurt like hell.

"What the actual fuck?" Alice cried.

"Yeah, so remember when I said that I would explain why I look weird? I guess I should have done that first. Now that I've been to hell, I'm not healed here in heaven. I'm healed in Hell, but more earth like. I have scars and stuff. But in Heaven, I'm like when I died. My back is broken too. My cat caused a wicked car crash, the damned thing. Literally, he's in Hell right now waiting for me."

Alice looked like if she could have barfed, she would have. Jess wished for a cloth and a bandage and began to fix Kat's arm again. She wiped up the blood, slipped the bone back under Kat's skin and wrapped it up with the bandage. When she was done, she pulled the sleeve back to cover the whole mess.

"That looks like it hurts," Alice said. "I guess it makes sense that you're broken here, but how do still have the Heaven glitter?"

"Oh, yeah. That's not Heaven glitter. It's strip club glitter. Fucking shit followed me to the afterlife."

"Um…ok," Alice said.

"So not a kindergarten teacher then…Let's get moving," Jess said and led the way out the door.

Night had fallen in Heaven as they stepped out of Alice's house. Jess and Alice didn't need any sleep, no one did in Heaven, but Kat was exhausted. Her back brace helped, but not all the way, and the effort to not just keep upright, but not do a zombie shuffle was becoming tedious. Her arm was killing her too. Kat was getting anxious to get back to Hell. Her fatigue was clouding her thoughts.

Kat needed two hands to spread the seed. One to hold the sack and one to throw it on the ground, but she found that her bad arm was nearly useless. She could still operate it, but the pain made it difficult. Jess saw her struggle and took the sack from her hands, with a look of sympathy that melted Kat's heart. She wondered if she had met Jess before escaping Heaven, she would have wanted to leave at all. She handed the sack to Alice, who began dumping it on the ground.

Kat was moving as fast as she could to the portal. She no longer cared all that much if she had to redo her face and stuff if she went into the portal and then back in Heaven. She wanted to rest her body. Her memories of her life had become misty, but she didn't think she had ever felt as tired or as much pain. Kat and Jess had pulled ahead of her, they were chatting away. Alice had been a librarian from what she could hear. But their voices began to fade. She sat down on a patch of grass to rest. She wanted to call out to them and let them know she'd be right there. She was sure if she had just a little break, she would be able to catch up, and didn't want to worry them. She closed her eyes for just a moment.

The sound of whispering voices woke her up. It was still dark so she thought she couldn't have been out very long. She looked up expecting Alice and Jess, but instead saw the tall, big boobed, redheaded angel. The very one who had been such an ass to Alice. She was alone at least but staring at her. She just smirked and walked away.

Only a few moments later, Alice and Jess came running toward her.

"Oh no. I'm so sorry," Jess said. "We just got to talking and thought you were right behind us. Are you alright?"

"I'm fine," Kat lied. "I just wanted to sit here on the grass for a few. Take in the scenery."

"Sure…" Alice said, and Kat liked that this one had a nose for bullshit. She was holding several more sacks of seed. She stuffed as many as she could into her pockets and she and Jess bracketed Kat and helped her to her feet. Kat bit her tongue to keep from grunting, then did anyway.

"Let's get you back into the portal to rest and be healed for a little while. I'll come back with my stuff to fix you up again. In the morning. The donuts will be here by then, and we can start phase two of operation 'Heaven sucks donkey balls'," Jess said. "We'll spread the seed until then."

"Jess wants to drop it from drones," Alice added. "You rest, we got this."

Kat only smiled. She couldn't think of anything other than getting back to the portal. She thought she might go all the way to Hell. With their help, getting back to the portal was relatively easy. They helped her through, and a few seconds later Satan showed up. Alice saw him just inside the portal and screamed. Jess clamped a firm hand around her mouth.

"Well, that was rude. I'm not that ugly," Satan laughed, and Alice began to moan around Jess' hand.

"He takes a little getting used to, to but he's cool I swear," Kat said. She was intact and her face and hair had returned to normal. Her exhaustion came with her though.

Alice calmed down some and said quietly, "I'm sorry, it's just that…"

"I'm fucking hideous, I know," Satan said. Kat heard the hurt through his jovial tone.

He plucked Kat off her feet and whisked her away to Hell.

14

"Tell me all about Heaven," Satan said with his large chin in the palms of his hands and his elbows on Kat's scratched kitchen table. Two steaming cups of coffee sat on either side of a big plate of golden donuts with sparkly icing. Kat had already had three. She didn't know if they just tasted better to her in Hell, or if he had improved on the recipe. She suspected the latter. "Did you see Jesus? God? Tell me everything…" He was almost whining.

Satan was wearing a black velour jumpsuit, much like his others. Ill fitting, it clung in all the wrong places. He was wearing a black matching beanie. She had never seen him wear a hat before. It stretched over his horns in an unappealing way, but Kat thought that he must be trying to cover them up. He didn't mention it, and she didn't expect him to, given his status as the ruler of Hell, but she thought Alice's reaction to him the day before had really upset him. He also looked like he might have put on a little eyeliner.

Satan had brought her all the way to her home, where she found Lucifer, Buster, and her knight in shining demon skin Amon. He made her dinner of roasted chicken (slightly overcooked) and mashed potatoes (only a tad lumpy). Then he tucked her in as only a demon lover could. He left after she fell asleep satisfied and doubly exhausted, wedged in between her cats. She didn't mind as he had Jess' cat Echo waiting for him at his house.

Echo had been fairly happy in Hell, but once she contacted her previous human, she became aggressively needy. Amon thought it best if he watched her at his house where there were no other cats until Jess made it down. He had brought her to Kat's house first, but Echo wasn't impressed by Lucifer's butthole and kept trying to get under the sofa. She mellowed out when he was there to take care of her. Amon wasn't much of a cat kind of demon, but he abided by the laws of Hell to be kind to all creatures. At least that is what he told Kat, but she wasn't sure she believed him. She once caught him rolling on the floor playing with Lucifer as if he were another cat, certainly giving her the impression that he was a cat kind of demon. She figured he didn't want to soil his tough-demon reputation. But he was as soft as they came, figuratively speaking.

Kat told Satan all about Heaven. How they had run into Jesus and that the bird seed seemed to be working fabulously. She told him about how it seemed that they were now hiding the most nefarious of the forgiven and that the administrative office was pushing the disinformation that any shit talking would be heard and reported. Typical God propaganda he had said. She also told him about the pain and sitting down in the grass. She had forgotten all about the whispering angel that had brought her out of her cat nap. Satan listened to all of it, while sipping his coffee and eating his donuts.

"You don't have to go back if you don't want to Kat," he said when she finished. "Your two new friends seem like they can handle it. Just meet them at the portal and help them from there." He looked worried. His eyeliner, she had become sure that's what it was, as she sat across from him, emphasized the concern in his eyes.

"Nope. They trusted me when they didn't have to. I owe it to them to see this through," she said. Kat had taken one of his huge hands in both of hers. An attempt to comfort the Prince of Darkness. "I got this. Besides, I'm already dead. What is there to be afraid of? Pain? Shithead angels? Nope. I'm doing this." She left out the part of maybe not being able to return to Hell. That was her real fear, but she had confidence that Satan would come get her if that happened. That confidence helped to squash that anxiety, if not completely eliminate it.

"Lemmy, I love you Kat. Hell is lucky to have you."

They finished up as Amon knocked on the door, he didn't wait for her to answer, just opened it and walked in.

"Hey there lover, how'd you sleep?" Amon swept her up in his arms and kissed her deeply.

"Wonderfully," she was only partially lying. Lucifer simply refused to get off of her pillow, and so she spent most of the night with pussy in her face and fur tickling her nose. Buster was content to sleep at her feet.

"Kat, are you ready to lick ass and take names?' Lucifer came bounding out of the living room. He saw Amon and turned around to show him his butthole.

"Put that away. And, I doubt I'll do any ass licking in Heaven," Kat giggled. She didn't want to correct the furball. He had made a valiant attempt to hide his own worry and be supportive.

"I'll lick your ass double when you get back!" Satan said.

Kat picked up Lucifer and snuggled him under her chin, "Be good. I'll be home soon."

She put Lucifer down and went to the sofa to scratch Buster's pretending-to-be-apathetic head between his ears. To his utter horror, she then bent down to plant a quick kiss on the spot she had just been petting. He closed his eyes, and for one brief moment, only a fraction of a second brief, Buster looked happy.

Amon's motorcycle was waiting just outside her door. She climbed onto the back of it, and he started the engine.

"Parker has the donuts waiting for you! Godspeed Kat!" Satan called as they sped off.

The sky was bright in Hell that morning. Or as bright as Hell ever gets. It hadn't rained in a little while, and the ground was dry. But the foliage was nothing short of gorgeous. She watched the people weeding and tending their gardens, planters, and yards as they rode past. The park was packed full of fanged rabbits and demon squirrels doing whatever it was that fanged rabbits and demon squirrels did. The tables were full of people playing chess at the little concrete tables. Kat had never played chess, wasn't really a fan of games at all. But considering the mostly cerebral inhabitants of Hell, the scientists, deep thinkers, Kat thought that Chess really was Hell's game.

They were almost to the Lake of Fire and the portal as they passed Hell's City Hall. Out in front, there were several people with their hands and heads in wooden stocks that had been painted black. Behind them stood a long line of Hell's inhabitants all of them wearing pointy toed boots. One demon was handing them out at the end of the line, while another directed them as their turns came. Kat cringed as she watched each person get their turn to kick the prisoners in the ass with their boots. A third demon took each used pair of boots, and a fourth brought those to the first demon at the back of the line. Efficient ass kicking.

Kat cringed as she heard one of the pointy toes land in the ass of a pudgy bald guy with a thud and a pathetic yelp. Amon must have felt her tense up because he said, "Advertising execs." Kat didn't cringe the next time she heard a yelp.

They got to the portal where Parker was waiting, just where Satan said they would be. The demon had a cart filled with pink bakery boxes. They were grinning as they bowed to Kat and Amon. Kat thought the portal was a little chilly this time as she walked through it. The candles still lit up as she walked, but the chill felt new.

Jess and Alice were waiting at the other end. Both wearing huge smiles. And they weren't alone. Kat counted around twenty other angels in all.

"We found some like-minded people," Jess said with a wicked wink, and an even more wicked smile. "Fruit consumption has dropped dramatically."

"Wow. I can't believe no one noticed the poop though," Kat returned her smile.

"It's all white and sparkly. Pretty much like everything in Heaven. It just blends in," Alice said. "We spread all of the rest of the seed last night."

"Jesus has been preaching and plenty of people have been listening. There are still plenty that could use the donuts though," Jess said. "I have my bag of tricks and am ready to do you up again."

Kat sighed an inadvertent sigh and stepped through pushing the cart of donuts. She turned to blow a kiss to Amon who held up two fingers in a 'V' and stuck his tongue in between them in response.

Jess who was so excited, she was practically vibrating said, "Ok, so I've been thinking about how to get people to try the donuts. Why would anyone be giving out stuff when all you have to do is wish for it?"

The giant hole in the plan became apparent to Kat then. *Why would anyone be giving anything away in Heaven? Duh....*

"But now that the effects of the stupid fruit have worn off, people are discovering boredom," Jess beamed. "And some of them are beginning to try to take up hobbies. Mine is baking," she said with a perfectly sly wink. Somehow her smile got bigger.

"I get it. Perfect. I can't say I've met an amateur baker or cook that wasn't always trying to push their creations on everyone around them." Kat remembered a stripper that she had danced with who was working her way through culinary school. Every other week she brought in something for people to try. Usually baked goods of some sort. Kat remembered it always tasted pretty good but sometimes looked like a mess. "Good fucking job Jess! I checked on Echo, by the way, she's good."

Jess' eyes teared up for only a second, then she yelled to the small crowd, "Each of you take a box. Jesus will be ready to speak soon, let's hand them out there."

The other angels did as they were told, and with Alice in the lead, began to walk away. All smiles and giggles. Jess turned toward Kat and motioned for her to lift her robe. Jess once again braced her back and bandaged her arm. She then set to work on her face and hair. It didn't take as long as it had the first time.

"Alright, let's go," Jess admiring her handiwork. She had come a long way since the frustrated state Kat had found her in. Heaven seemed to have dimmed her light, but her mission for Hell had reignited it.

They made their way to the platform, where Jesus was already preaching. Kat heard Jess' words spill from his passionate, but vapid lips. Most of the audience had a donut in their hands. They were listening intently. Jesus usually had an attentive crowd, but this one was a little different. They hung on every word, but rather than the reverence and groupie-like moans of extasy, Kat heard a bit of confusion. Then understanding. It reminded her of the orgy she had incited her first time in Heaven, but this time it was epiphanies and not orgasms that roared through the angels. Once again, she smiled at a well-executed if not well-planned scheme.

Jess and Alice and the rest of their new friends were chatting among themselves. Jesus having impressed himself with his own preaching began to repeat himself, but louder. As it drew more attention, Kat thought it might be a good time to see her dad again.

She pulled Jess out of the group. Jess was holding a pink box. When she noticed it was empty, she wished it away, there are no garbage cans in Heaven as there is no garbage.

"I'm going to go get my dad. You look like you have things handled here."

"I do," Jess said. "Don't take too long. We've run out of donuts and have a few hundred people to lead to the portal. You should be back to talk to them before we lead them through and on to Hell. We have to tell them exactly what's up."

"Definitely. I think we lose some of them, but transparency is imperative. I won't be long."

Kat walked as fast as her broken spine would allow her toward her dad's house. The sun was once again shining as it did in Heaven. It was warm and the ground inviting. It was sparklier than it had been, and she smiled because Heaven was literally covered in shit. She felt pain and fatigue, but the overall pleasantness bled through. Heaven still held for her an underlying current of dread and deceit, but a nice day was a nice day. She found herself humming as she walked. Carefully. She stopped humming when she realized she was humming the same Taylor Swift song that she had heard Jess humming. *Not today, Taylor Swift, not today...*

She reached her dad's house and knocked on the front door. She could hardly wait to tell him about all their success and her new friends. And to bring him to Hell of course.

"Dad!" She said when he opened the door. He hugged her tight while Beelzebub stood behind him. She followed him through the door where she promptly sat down on his sofa, relieving some of the pressure off of her back. Taking a page from the book of Jess, she began the rapid-fire retelling of her exploits since they had last spoken. He looked interested but also seemed to be waiting to talk. When she finally got all of her words out, she took a deep breath and said "Well?"

"Kathryn," a sense of dread warmed her belly with her father's use of her full name, "I have some news. I've gotten word that your mother is at the gates. She is waiting to speak with St Peter. The line is kind of long, as I guess there was some kind of pandemic on earth. A bit of a back log. The rumor is, too many people put their faith in God's hands, and not the doctors. Something about a monster called Big Pharma and a thing called the internet and 'influencers'." He paused to let her process a little. There was no bottle on his table this time. "They asked me to meet her at the Administrative building when she gets in." Kat had no doubt her mother would get in, tears streamed down her face. "I can't come with you right now Kat."

"I'll get her a donut. It will be ok. Give me a few minutes, I'll be back soon," Kat got up to leave. Her father walked her to the door.

"Kat, I'm not sure that will work. Maybe, give her some time to get used to being dead and stuff. Her faith has always been strong, and I bet even more so after both of us passed. We can't just pull the rug out from under her. It will take time for her to understand, Kat. And even then, she might not make the choice you want her to," he hugged her in his doorway.

"Ok, I understand. But I have to tell my friends that I can't go with them now. I need to be with my mom. If you're gone when I get back, I'll wait for you and mom here."

He shut the door and Kat wobble-ran through the gate and down the street. Tears streamed down her face. The paint that was pretending to be makeup ran down her cheeks, but she didn't care. She wanted to see her mom. Her memories from earth returned with painful brilliance. Satan had granted her permission to contact her mother on earth to ease her mother's mind, to free her from the suffering of thinking her daughter was spending an eternity in a lake of fire. She could hardly wait to show her mom the real Lake of Fire, and it's funny birds and bunnies.

Kat was so lost in her thoughts, emotions, and desperation to keep her spine from crumpling that she didn't notice the busty redheaded angel coming up behind her until she heard her name. Well, not her name, but what the assholes in Heaven called her.

"I knew that was you...Kathy." The angel sneered.

Kat stopped and turned to face her. A great come back locked and loaded and ready to fire, but before the epic burn left her lips the angel spoke again, "I come bearing a gift from God, you flippin' whore."

Kat began to giggle as she pictured a hooker doing back flips. Her giggle died in her throat as the beautiful angel wore the ugliest smile she had ever seen. She lifted her perfect hand and pointed a perfect finger at Kat. A hot white flame spewed forth and engulfed Kat sending her to the ground. She was on fire. Her hair went first as the flame went from the top of her head to her bare feet taking everything down to her skin with it. She collapsed to the ground as she heard the sound of the redheaded angel's footsteps retreat.

For Kat, the light of Heaven went dark.

15

Kat awoke to the site of the most beautiful angel she had ever seen. And she had seen a lot of angels. This one looked like her mother. Except much too young. A soft glow framed her face as she held a cool damp cloth her forehead. Kat figured she must be dreaming.

Then Kat realized she wasn't dreaming. She was dead. And in Heaven. *Fuck.*

"Kathryn, I'm here," Kat's mother said.

"Mom?"

"Yes. You're ok. You had some sort of accident. But you're all better now. Sit up and have some tea. I can get you a donut if you like too."

Oooo…Donut! Kat thought, but then said with a scowl, "Tea is just fine."

Her mother looked confused but handed her a cup of tea. She knew she was still in Heaven at the sight of her mother, but had it not been for that, the fact that she didn't have to blow on her tea to cool it gave it away. The temperature was perfect for sipping. Kat sipped it and it was perfection laced with resentment.

Kat was in her father's house, sitting on his plaid sofa with her now healed arm on the armrest. She was wearing a Heaven robe. But not Lyla's old one, a brand new one. One that was made just for her. It was covered in sparkles. Not the usual heavenly sparkles either. But a more aggressive version. And to add that special something, 'Kathy' was emblazoned on the breast of it in a bright pink glittery thread.

"I think they added that special for you. I tried to tell them that your name was Kathryn not Kathy, but they said you liked that better. Heaven must have changed you dear." Her mother's eyes had gone glassy with tears. But Kat didn't think they were sad tears, her mother was happy to see her. Tears of joy. The very first tears of joy she had ever seen in Heaven. She thought about telling her that God was just fucking with her but didn't have the heart. Probably not any other organs either.

Kat felt pretty good. Great in fact. Especially for someone who had just been smited by a vengeful God. She sipped more tea as her mother watched her. She was happy to see her mother but was finding the angel version of her almost painful to look at. Her father had died so young that when she saw his younger self in Heaven it wasn't as jarring. Kat kept her eyes down as she sipped. Whatever had happened to her, she thought it was some kind of burning light. Not quite fire, but she remembered it burned like crazy. But she felt none of it now.

She reached up to feel her hair. Not the short bob that Jess had given her, but her own long, thick, and shiny locks. Her back and arm were healed, she wiggled a bit in her seat and felt something weird. Maybe not weird. But nothing. She felt nothing between her legs. She hopped up off the sofa and ran to the little bathroom where she slipped off the hideous robe.

She expected to find a smooth lump between her legs and found no surprise there. The nipple-less bumps she had instead of breasts she did not expect. *What the actual fuck?* She stared at her perfect reflection in the mirror and wanted to puke. Not a mark, not a blemish, not a nipple or clitoris. She wanted to die. Again.

Cool fucking trick, she thought. *Now I actually want to put the robe back on.* Kat pulled the robe back over her head, and walked as calmly as she could back out to the living room where her mother waited.

"Where's dad?" Kat felt confident that she was masking the alarm in her voice. Her mother's response told her she had succeeded.

"He is at the Administration office. They are going to give us a special house. One where we can be as a family. Oh Kat, isn't it wonderful?"

Kat didn't think it was any kind of wonderful and all kinds of fucked up.

"Wonderful. Did you have a nice death?" Kat paused. "I mean, it wasn't too bad?"

"Oh no. Died in my sleep. Aneurysm. Other than the long wait at the gate, it wasn't bad. St Peter is such a nice man." Her mother smiled and she wanted to puke again. She didn't think her mother had heard about her exchange with the royal asshat who sat at the pearly gates. Which was probably a good thing.

A thick silence settled over the small living room. Beelzebub laid by the couch, not helping at all, unless you count the occasional dog snore. Kat just didn't know what to say. Her mother hadn't approved of her life on earth, and that was only the part she knew about. Kat couldn't help but wonder if her mother had known all of it, the one-night stands, the light pickpocketing of her strip club customers, and her total lack of belief in God, she might not even be talking to her right now. Although, Kat was grateful that she had so far been spared the 'I told you so' about the God thing.

Her mother seemed to feel the same way. Sensing the giant mastodon in the room but not wanting to address it. The awkward and very pregnant silence was much less awkward than the conversation they were both avoiding. Kat loved her mother, and she knew that her mother loved her. Kat wanted nothing more than to explain to her all she had learned since she died but didn't even know where to start. She simply couldn't think of a polite way to tell her mother that she had devoted her life to a malignant narcissist and His lies. Thankfully, her father was there to rescue them both.

Beelzebub began to wag his tail before they heard Kat's father open the door.

"Louise! You're going to love the house," he said as he entered. "Oh Kat, you're awake. How are you feeling?"

"Perfect," Kat said with a fake smile. She needed to talk with her father alone but had no clue how to accomplish that. But once again, he came through.

Kat's father kissed her mother on the cheek, "Our new place is grand, you are really going to love it. It's exactly what you wanted." The look of pure contentment on her mother's face broke her heart. "But there's one thing. It's almost perfect, but there are a few things that I want Kat and I to get in order before I take you there. It won't take long. Can you wait here?"

"Of course!" Louise said. "I will find something to stay occupied." She turned to a large bookshelf, where Kat knew that her mother wouldn't find anything remotely offensive. She kissed her goodbye and headed out the door with her father. Beelzebub followed behind them.

As soon as they were out of the gate Kat said, "What the hell happened? I remember the redheaded angel lighting me up, then waking up on the couch. How much does mom know?"

"Mom doesn't know anything other than you had an accident and were taking a deep nap on the sofa. I heard the noise outside and found you burned to a crisp. When I brought you inside, you healed but stayed asleep. I went to retrieve your mother. They told me to take her back to my house, but to come back right after I got her settled. I think they wanted you to wake up to her."

"So, mom doesn't know about the hell thing?"

"She doesn't. She thinks you got into Heaven…and stayed here."

Kat was relieved, but that hadn't been her biggest worry. She had disappointed her mother before, and that she could deal with. Kat looked down at her censored and sanitized perfect body and wondered if she were here for good now. Not to mention her friends and all the people they were trying to help.

"What does God know?" Kat was afraid of the answer.

"A lot. But not everything. He knows you got back in but doesn't quite know how. He figured you wanted back in and granted it. My guess is that you are going to be the new poster child for His mercy and salvation. So, your mother will probably find out about the Hell thing."

"Super," Kat said and rolled her eyes.

"I don't think they have any idea about the birds or the donuts or the portal or any of that."

"That is good. But dad," Kat was relieved that the mission didn't seem compromised, but she still had one burning question. "Am I stuck here?"

They were walking down a beautiful street that boasted houses a little bigger than the ones she had seen, but otherwise the same. Her dad stopped in front of one of them and opened the gate.

"Kat, I don't know. They told me that I am to keep an eye on you here in Heaven, but I suspect you'll be watched pretty closely by others. That's why they won't grant you your own house. You are to be with your mother and me. At least that's what I got from talking to the angel they assigned to me, God is gloating about your return. I doubt He'll let you leave again. It's pretty good PR for Him."

"But if the portal is still around, then I can just go through again," Kat sounded skeptical, even to herself. She had learned a few hard lessons about taking anything for certain in Heaven or Hell.

"Maybe, but if you do, I think we can count on that being the last portal ever between Heaven and Hell. If you try to leave, someone is going to notice."

Kat knew he was right. Even if she got through, there was no way they would get away with making another no matter how many physicists they had in Hell. Fool God once, and you get burned to a crisp and lose your nipples, fool God twice and it was anybody's guess what the bastard would do. She would have to get as many people as possible out that wanted to leave before she could even try to leave herself. Kat needed to find Jess and Alice. That also meant that she would probably have to leave the people that really deserved to be in Hell, here in Heaven. The blood thirstiest of Satan's minions would be terribly disappointed.

They opened the door to their new family home. It was lovely. Kat hated it. Her whole life she fought against conformity. From a young age, she valued her independence over everything else. Pretty much why she became a stripper. If there had been any gift that she had been given by religion, it was her determination to make her own choices. That a god, any god, would demand devotion and worship in exchange for the privilege of not being burned for eternity, smacked of emotional manipulation. So much so, that she had been unable to believe in His existence at all. All she learned in church was that she wasn't the kind of girl to be extorted by an imaginary deity. Finding that deity to be real after her death, didn't change her opinion of Him at all. A manipulative asshat was a manipulative asshat. And now, she might be stuck with such an asshat forever.

"What is it we needed to do for mom?" Kat asked. She figured she would get her mother settled before looking for Jess and Alice.

"Nothing. It's all perfect. There's not a damned thing we could do to make it any better," her father said sadly.

Kat took a quick look around at what might be her prison for all eternity. There were two bedrooms. In her parent's room, there were two single beds separated by a nightstand on which sat a bible. Apparently even sexless cuddling between a married couple was frowned upon in Heaven. A bathroom done in cream and pink and that lacked a toilet down a short hallway was between a second bedroom. Her bedroom she assumed. She didn't want to go in at all, but knew she would have to at some point, so she took a tentative step inside.

It wasn't like the gawdy porno set her first Heaven bedroom had been. She closed her eyes and tried wishing it that way, but when she opened them, she saw that nothing had changed. God had apparently limited her wishing capabilities. If she had any at all. She closed her eyes and wished she had a cup of coffee, and one appeared in her hand. She dropped it on the floor out of sheer spite, where it disappeared before it could land and give her any satisfaction by making a mess.

She stepped into her new room. Purple. And turquoise. She had a single bed like her parents, complete with a bible on the nightstand. Her bible was covered in sparkles she noticed with a grimace. She did see that she had a bookshelf and was amazed to see it full of titles she would love if she hadn't loved already when she was alive. It was full of horror, smut, crime, dark humor. And one book on manners. *Ha Ha*, she thought. But before she got her hopes up, she remembered poor Alice's bookshelf. She pulled a Clive Barker novel off the shelf and opened it to a random page. It looked like gibberish. Mostly because it was gibberish. The text was that of the bible. She put it back on the shelf and didn't bother looking at the other books. She knew that they were just the bible in good literature's clothing. She wondered if they might have been all the different edited versions of it, maybe some of the missing books that had been conveniently left out by the humans that put the whole thing together. But she figured her bookshelf wasn't big enough to hold all of those. She also knew without looking that the only book on her shelf in Heaven that hadn't been replaced with the bible was the book on manners. If there was one thing God was really good at, it was creating a personal Hell. Kat thought she might have preferred stocks and pointy boots in her ass, over this travesty. If only she had gone into advertising instead of stripping.

She met her dad back out in the living room. She tried to hide the utter dejection she was feeling. But he saw through it.

"I'm sorry Kat. But we have forever to figure it out."

She hugged him, "Dad, I need to find my friends."

"I know honey. Please be careful though. You're not going to move through Heaven unnoticed anymore. I'll go get your mom. Don't be too long, she'll be waiting for you."

She nodded and thought, *great, I have a curfew.* They walked together down the path to the street and went in separate directions after they went through the gate. Kat didn't know where to find Jess or Alice. She wanted to go toward the portal but had no idea what kind of surveillance she might be under. She decided to head in the direction of Jesus's platform instead.

The day was perfect…again. Kat decided she hated perfect. But without the pain and fatigue, she couldn't help but feel physically good. Her mind, however, was screaming. The warmth of cobblestones was a massage on her feet. The air was clean and crisp but not cold. The birds and squirrels frolicked in the glitter-shit covered trees. The whole place reflected the sun as if it were a big magical disco ball.

As she walked, she saw something she hadn't seen before. A giant billboard. For the life of her, or death of her maybe, she couldn't understand what purpose a billboard might serve in Heaven. But this one had her face on it. Above her head floated a halo, like the one that floated over her head as she looked up. Not Satan's halo, but God's. The text underneath her angelic smile, read: Kathy, proof of God's mercy. If she can be saved, anyone can. *What a fucking dick,* Kat thought.

16

And there she was. Her ultimate punishment was to be God's shining example of the saved wretch. Once lost, now found, and trapped. The subject of a holy PR campaign. Her mother would finally be proud of her. Kat wondered if they would tell the whole story. The angel orgy she had started, the gluttony, the semi-consensual sexual assault of Chad the hot-as-fuck-but-still-creepy admin angel and her ultimate escape and return. Kat hoped they wouldn't, but God's whole schtick was making shit up. So maybe she could convince her mom that it was just a holy embellishment? They had already done a lot to cover it up, even if some of the angels still knew. But now that it could be spun in God's favor, she thought it they would likely hype it up.

Still, she hoped that rather than tell her true story of getting into Heaven then getting out, they would tell inside the story of her life and how she had decided to beg for forgiveness in her last dying moments. They would likely leave out the part that she didn't believe one word of the prayer she had uttered under the extreme stress of knowing she was going to die. Of course, belief is kind of a funny thing. Kat wasn't sure how one would prove they really believed and weren't just pretending in case they might get sent to be tortured forever.

They would definitely leave out the filthy thoughts she had about the paramedic who held her as she died. But the story of her escape to Hell, and God granting her mercy and allowing her to come back would be too hard for Him to pass up. He gets to look like the good guy and driving home the lie that Hell is as bad as He's been saying. For the most part, she didn't really care who knew. She had long run out of fucks to give about what anyone thought of her. Except her mom. She had one very large fuck left to give about that.

If Kat found any comfort in this new insult, it was that her mother would be proud of her. At least until she heard about the escape part. It was a cold and bitter comfort that would be short lived. She had longed for her mother's approval on earth. But she knew that in order to gain it, she would have to don a façade that was anything but true. Her mother's vision of her was as unrealistic as the idea of a loving God that required pain and suffering on earth in order to avoid pain and suffering in the afterlife. The approval that would come from God's latest gaslighting job, would end up feeling empty. All Kat wanted was the truth. Simple honesty and the courage to say 'I don't know' rather than deceit and false happiness. What Kat wanted was Hell.

Kat heard Jesus before she saw him. She almost giggled as she recognized Jess' words come out of his mouth. He didn't seem to get what he was saying, simply enjoying the audience it brought. Kat saw what had to have been some hundred or so angels, hanging on his every word. A few of them had donuts in their hands. None of them were eating the fruit. She looked to the nearest tree to see if the uneaten fruit would be rotting on the ground. But then remembered that nothing rotted in Heaven. The sparklier than usual fruit simply hung there.

She looked for either Jess or Alice but saw neither. There were two angels handing out donuts, but she didn't recognize them. One of them, a blonde male saw her and frowned. While a little surprised by his reaction, she walked toward him anyway. He shut the top of the bakery box he was holding and brought it closer to his chest.

"Hey, I'm Kat. Do you know where Jess or Alice are?"

"I know who you are. I'm just handing out Jess' donuts for her. It's her latest project," he said, not offering his name.

Kat assuming that he was trying to maintain their cover, cupped her hands around her mouth and whispered to him, "I know. I'm the one that was helping them with the poo and the donuts. I ran into some trouble. I need to talk to them."

The blonde angel sneered at her and turned his back. Kat was confused, but only for a moment. Behind the platform was yet another billboard. This one had her on stage in her stripper garb, with the naughty bits blurred out, with the text "Kathy, filthy sinner. Bathed in the blood of Jesus and redeemed!' He didn't trust her now that she had been saved. The mission seemed alive and well though, and she wanted to be happy about that. But she wasn't sure how happy she could be if the cost was her eternal freedom.

Kat hung her head and walked away from the platform. She didn't know where to look for her friends, or if they would even talk to her. She didn't know if she would be able to talk to Amon or Satan ever again. And she was supposed to go home to her parents soon. Kat knew that Heaven was unpredictable. Pretty much everything in the afterlife had been. Nothing was guaranteed in a realm where the supernatural deity in charge could simply change the rules at will. Every word and commandment left open to selfish interpretation. But still, Kat found herself disappointed in her ability to control anything at all. She didn't get far before she heard someone call her name. Well not her name, but she knew they were referring to her.

"Hey look! It's her! Kathy!"

Kat looked toward the voice and saw a group of around ten angels staring at her. Getting stared at was something she was used to in life. In fact, it was her job. And in Heaven, she had gotten used to it to as the defiant pariah who simply refused to go with the flow. This staring was something different altogether. These angels who stared at her now, looked excited to see her. Not excited like the guys sitting at her tip rail in the strip club, more like a herd of groupies staring at a sweaty rockstar. Albeit pious, forcibly celibate groupies. They had their hands to their mouths as if she were some sort of celebrity, one petite brown-haired angel looked as if she were going to faint.

Kat waved and quickened her step, but the angel mob caught up with her. She didn't have much of a choice but to stop. And besides, she didn't really have anywhere to go. As soon as her legs stopped moving, she was surrounded.

"Kathy! You're an inspiration, a saint. Oh, the souls you'll save," a very tall and very pale angel said to her.

Kat was confused, "Um, thank you. But what do you mean?"

The pale angel replied, "God's grace has made you humble," and bowed her head.

Kat only became more confused. She'd been called all sorts of things, but not humble was not one of them.

The tiny angel finally found her voice, "The good you will do on earth. God has chosen you to return to deliver his message of hope."

"What the actual fuck?" Kat said. She had not intended to say it out loud. The group of angels gasped in unison at her curse word.

"It's ok," a dark-skinned angel said to the rest of them. "Her flaws are what will guide the wicked to their eternal salvation."

The crowd began to line up in front of her, each one taking her hand and planting a kiss on it with a bow, before peeling off so the next one could pay their respects. Kat was still confused but more was becoming clear. It sounded like she was going to be the next of God's martyrs on earth. Just like Jesus. Was God was going to crucify her and use her to collect more souls for his holy un-paradise? Kat thought a dip in the lake of fire, or minions tossing her severed head around would be more fun.

Just as she thought the line was getting shorter, more angels added to it. She could still hear Jesus preaching from his platform, but it sounded like he was winding down. She looked toward the platform, and saw the angels there, including the guy that had been handing out Jess' special donuts looking at the spectacle she was making with disgust. Normally that would have pissed her off, but she was actually relieved. Those who weren't rushing over to kiss her hand and gush over her newfound salvation, weren't buying the lie. Her mission was at least partially intact. She might be totally screwed, but at least some people were getting a chance at the truth. There were some that would get the choice. They began to peel off and head in the direction of the portal. She hoped Jess and Alice or one of their recruits would be there to help them through the portal if that's what they chose.

The line wasn't getting any shorter, and Kat realized that if she didn't say something, she would be here forever. Or at least until they sent her back to earth or whatever fucked up plan God had come up with. She had to give it to Him, this was far worse than anything she had seen Satan dream up. God was a dick, but a creative one.

Kat didn't think there was anything she could do but play the roll until she knew more. She allowed one more kiss, then said, "My sheep," she didn't think that was right, lamb maybe? But she rolled with it, "I must leave you now and go to be with my parents. "Stay sparkly," she said as she pointed at them with her hands mimicking pistols. Then Kat bowed, and as she dipped down toward the ground, she looked up to see if her act was working. It seemed to be. The angels, looking dejected but satisfied that they had gotten close to her. When she stood up straight, they were all bowing still but giving her space. She began to walk toward her new home, giving her best Miss America wave until she was out of sight.

Kat couldn't cry, or barf, or die, but wished she could have done any of those things. Anything at all to get some relief from the overwhelming emotion she felt. Above all, she felt stupid. She tried to take on God. She had fought her way into Hell and had made it, why she ever thought that she could fight him again and win was beyond her. She didn't know if she would ever get to talk to or see Satan, Amon, or her new friends. She tried to take solace in that she was pretty sure that Jess and Alice would be able to get out of here, even if she couldn't. As Kat neared her parent's home, she thought she might just get herself a bottle of whisky. Or since she was incapable of puking, tequila. With that thought she wondered if Jose Quervo was in Heaven or Hell.

Kat had her head down as she walked. The sun was on its way down and the sunset was nothing short of amazing, but she longed for the blood-soaked evenings in Hell. Filled with a sense of loss and entrapment, Kat tried to put on a face that would hide all of that for her mother. Her dad might see through it, but her mother was happy. And Kat didn't see any reason to make her feel otherwise. She didn't bother to knock since it was going to be her home forever, she just walked in. Her parents were sitting in the living room and didn't notice her at first. But when they did, her mother got up to hug her. She was obviously excited.

"Kat! My angel. Why didn't you tell me?" Her mother said.

"I only just found out myself."

"It's more than I ever could have hoped for. I knew when you came to me after your death that God had forgiven you, but I would have never guessed He had this purpose for you."

"It's pretty great," Kat said.

Her dad had his eyes to the floor.

"I think I'm ready for a margarita," Kat said as one appeared in her hand. She took a sip; it was a virgin. *Perfect.* She thought. God gave Satan Scientology; He gave her eternal sobriety and celibacy. If she had ever had any doubt who the real monster in this scenario was, it dissolved in that moment. "You know, I think I would like to do some reading in my room," Kat couldn't bear to look at her mother anymore. She had no intention of reading, but she needed to be alone.

"Kat, the administration office left you a note. I put it on your pillow," her dad said. She couldn't read his tone, but she sensed something off. She suspected the note was from God or one of His pious minions explaining what His plan was for her.

"Thanks dad," Kat said, trying on a fake smile for her mother. Her mother smiled back. She padded slowly down the hallway to her room. She saw the note on her pillow, but she had no desire to read it. She would have to at some point.

There was something else in her room that hadn't been there before also. A music player with headphones. Something kind of like an iPod she thought. Just another cruel joke she figured. It was probably loaded with Creed or Amy Grant. If she turned that shit on, she would probably barf. Stomach or not.

Kat laid down on her purple bed, casting the note aside. It was pink with her name spelled out in glitter. Well not her name. She closed her eyes and wished for sleep. To her astonishment, it came. She didn't dream, but when she woke, the sun had come up, and she realized that God had granted her that. That small bit of unconsciousness, a small reprieve from the hell that was Heaven. She found herself just a little bit grateful to God. But only a little.

Kat picked up the note that had been left. She had been able to sleep, which hadn't done much for her state of mind. She still felt trapped, helpless, and with the exception of her father, utterly alone. But she figured she should look at the damned note. Kat turned it over in her hand and noticed with curiosity that some of the glitter had fallen into her lap. Glitter in Heaven was embedded in everything. You couldn't rub or wash it off. The glitter from the envelope was like stripper glitter, the stuff that was forever simply because it was mobile. And even when you thought it was gone, it showed up in the most inconvenient of places. With a sigh, she opened the envelope. It read:

Kat, please enjoy the music I have left for you. We'll talk soon.

Her heart leapt but crashed back down an instant later. She looked at the note which, if she was correct, had to be destroyed immediately. She suspected, or hoped rather, that it came from Amon. She waited a moment to see if it would simply burn up on its own. When it didn't, she put the corner in her mouth and bit off a piece and began to chew. She didn't dare wish for a glass of water, lest it draw attention. So, she proceeded to chew the rest of the note and swallow it. She brushed the glitter off of her chin when she was finished.

Kat picked up the headphones and put them on. There were only two buttons on the player. Stop and start. And immediately regretted the decision to push the play button as Creed's 'Can you take me higher' began to assault her ears. She wanted to throw it across the room but resisted the urge. And listened for just another moment. And then music began to play backwards. She was not at all surprised to discover that Creed still sucked but slightly less backwards. The unfortunate song kept playing, and she kept listening. And then faintly, almost too faint to hear, was Satan's voice. It said, "Kat, hold tight, we got you. I promise." When the message finished, the song began to play forward again, and she took off the headphones. As she set the player down on the nightstand, it caught fire and disappeared in a puff of crimson smoke. She felt a little foolish for ingesting the note, as it probably would have done the same. Or maybe not.

Satan was probably laughing in Hell at the thought of her eating it.
And in that moment, Kat was almost happy in Heaven.

17

Knowing that Satan hadn't forsaken her, made Kat smile. A real actual smile. She didn't know how or when but just knowing that he was trying meant more than she could express. She had no idea how the player had gotten through or if there would be another message. Nor did she know how to get a message to Satan. Kat got up and went into the living room where she found her parents having coffee.

Her mother beamed at her over a perfect cup of coffee, "Good morning, Kathryn!"

"Good morning mom," Kat said, still wearing her genuine smile.

"Morning Kat," her father said. He had a gleam in his eye, she couldn't quite place. "Would you like some coffee?"

The offer was, of course, a formality. All she had to do was wish for a cup. Which she did before sitting down at their breakfast table. It sat in a nook with a large bay window that faced the street. Outside was another sickeningly beautiful day. Kat wished for a bagel, purely out of spite. She let it sit on the plate with just the right amount of cream cheese, not getting too cold, and never stale.

"Have you had a chance to walk around outside mom? It's pretty cool." Kat thought she was making a good show of sincerity. Her ultimate objective was to get to talk to her dad alone. She didn't know if he knew the origin of the note, or about the music player or not. But she really needed to know.

"I haven't, but your father and I were going to do that. Would you come with us?"

Not what she wanted, but she had to say, "Yes mom. That would be great."

"What did the note you received say? Or can you share it?" Her mother asked.

"I think I need to keep it to myself," Kat lied. What else was she supposed to say, that Satan had given her a message through backwards music? That would go over like a loud fart in church.

Her father just looked intensely into his coffee mug. Kat sipped a little more coffee. Thankful that she could at least feel some effects from the caffeine, Kat got up and smoothed her robe. Her parents stood up and after wishing the table cleared, it was. The sunlight almost hurt her eyes it was so bright outside. Her mother held her head to the soft warm breeze, closed her eyes, and smiled. Kat's stomach turned. She knew she didn't want to stay. She knew that she would never be happy here, and while she wanted to tell her mother the truth, looking at her now, it seemed it would be cruel. Her mother had waited her whole life to get here. She had done everything right. She hadn't hurt people or exploited the idea of sin and redemption to simply accept forgiveness, as her daughter had done. Louise had done it the right way, she had legitimately earned her place in Heaven, and she would love it here. Her opinion might change if she found out the truth about God and all that. But if she never knew, she would be dwelling in her own paradise for eternity. Just without her only daughter. Kat had wanted to try and open her eyes, but looking at her now she didn't think she would have the heart. And not just literally.

As they walked down the warm cobblestone road, looking at all the little houses, some with angels in front of them, some were empty. All perfect. Her mother marveled at the trees and bushes, and sparkly fruit. Her mother waved at the other angels as she passed. She started to pull ahead a little from Kat and her dad. Kat noticed and began to slow down to allow more distance, her dad did the same, and soon her mother was out of ear shot.

Kat whispered just in case her mother could still hear her, "Dad, where did you get the note and the music player?"

"Jess gave me the note yesterday. She said she was from the admin office. I don't know anything about the music player. It's not from the administration office, is it?" Her dad whispered back.

"It's not." Kat wondered how much Jess knew about the smiting she took or any of that. "I have to find her."

"She didn't say anything else. Go now, while your mom is occupied. Just be back before dark."

Kat frowned at the last statement. *Just be back before dark*, Kat didn't want to be back at all. And now she wasn't just terrified of getting stuck in Heaven, but she might be looking at her own crucifixion on earth as well. She ran to catch up with her mother, who was still in her own world of bliss. If Kat found Jess and or Alice, she would try to leave and take them with her. Even if she just made it to the portal without them, she was going to dive headfirst into it if she could. This could be the last she saw of her mom. Forever.

"Hey mom," Louise turned to Kat wearing her heartbreaking smile. "I'm going to go hang with my friends. I'll be back for dinner," which Kat thought may or may not be a lie. She swept her mother into a much tighter and longer hug than was warranted, but if her mother thought it was weird, she didn't say. Just saying she would be home for dinner was weird in itself given they would never be hungry. So maybe her mother was adjusting to weird.

"Ok, Kathryn. Have fun!" Kat felt twelve again.

She hugged her father, and whispered in his ear, "I don't know if I'll be back dad." He pulled away and looked at her sadly. But nodded his head in understanding. She had thought that he might come with her, but now that her mom was here, she didn't think so. But she really couldn't know what he wanted. Only that she didn't want become martyr for a narcissistic deity. Kat turned and trotted away, before either of her parents saw the tears floating in her eyes. She loved them. But she couldn't handle the idea of getting stuck in Heaven. At least they would have each other, and that might really be enough for them.

She ran toward the portal, doing her best to avoid been seen by anyone. But when she came across a group of angels she slowed and waved as they swooned. More billboards had gone up, each one depicting one of her various sins. She passed one that showed her and Lucifer on Jesus' platform acting out the sin of gluttony. She laughed as she saw her bloated face covered in some unidentifiable goo, while Lucifer showed his blurred out ass to the disapproving crowd that had gathered. Good times *could* be had in Heaven, if only short lived.

She came to the small grouping of trees just beyond the portal and saw Jess walking toward her. Kat looked around and saw that mercifully, they were alone.

"Oh, thank Lemmy!" Kat said and instantly regretted her volume by the look on Jess' face.

"Shhhh…." Jess said, looking around alarmed. "You're in a bunch of trouble Kat."

"They're going to crucify me, I know. I…."

Jess interrupted, "No probably not. But that's not the thing…."

Now Kat interrupted, "What do you mean probably not?"

"I told Satan, and he said, God isn't going to send you to earth. He said you'll probably show up on a piece toast or a dog's ass if anything."

Kat cocked her head and frowned, "A dog's ass?"

"It's a bit complicated, but I don't have time now. If anyone sees me talking to you our mission might be compromised. Just get your ass to the portal and get the fuck out of here. I've gotten a few hundred out, and Alice and I are ready to go to. I think we've done all we can here." Jess paused for a moment, just staring at her. "Gosh, you're pretty."

"Thanks, but it's all smoke and mirrors. Ok, I'm ready," but Kat wasn't sure she was. She had wanted to get some of the assholes out of here and leaving now meant she had failed there. Although, most of her apprehension came from the thought of leaving her parents. She hadn't even had a chance to talk to her aunt Judy since returning either. Kat didn't see much of an alternative though. It was now or never. Probably literally.

Kat took a deep breath and began to run for the portal. Jess ran just ahead of her. Soon the portal was in sight. Alice was standing at the entrance, waving to them. Kat took a quick look around to make sure that no one was watching them. There were alone. Jess got to the portal first and she waited with Alice for Kat to get there too. They stood on either side of the portal with their hands out like a couple of game show spokesmodels showcasing the grand prize. Kat appreciated the gesture but stopped short of going through.

"You guys go first," Kat said.

"Are you sure?" Alice said, looking concerned.

"Definitely. I'll be right behind you. Promise," Kat held two fingers to her heart, and backed up a little to let them go inside. They both walked through and to the other side easily. The motioned once again for her to follow. Kat held her breath and took a step toward the portal.

Voices, well a voice, blew through the thicket of trees that hid the entrance to the portal. The redheaded big tittied angel was leading her legions of followers. She hadn't seen Kat, but she was getting closer. Kat took a few steps back again, closed her eyes and leaped into the entrance of the portal.

Her perfect heaven nose was squashed up against an invisible screen as she was bounced back into Heaven. She had felt no pain after the redheaded angel had burnt her up. But she felt all of this. She felt as if she had been struck by a semi-truck. She looked down to see if she were as bleeding or as broken as she felt, but nothing. She was intact. Her feelings were only feelings, really awful shitty feelings, but feelings just the same. The pain was far more intense than anything she had felt on earth or in hell.

Kat could hear the angel and her minions getting closer. She stood up gracefully and the pain began to subside. She wondered if she should try again, maybe there was just a door handle or something she had missed. *Did I push when I should have pulled?* But she dismissed the stupid thought as soon as it came. The portal wasn't for her anymore. She turned to wave goodbye to her friend with tears in her eyes. But as she raised her unbroken arm, she saw that the portal, and her friends were gone.

Kat crumpled to the ground, as the redheaded angel began to call her name. *That's not my fucking name*, she thought.

18

"**K**athy!" the redheaded angel called. "Oh, whatever are you doing on the ground? You have fans to meet!"

Kat stood up with the thought or hope that Satan knew her plight and was already on his way. She brushed herself off, although she wasn't dirty. The world around her sparkled with malice and bird shit.

"Elicia," one of the other angels said, "She's even more beautiful than you said she would be." There were around twenty angels surrounding her.

Elicia, Kat thought with a grimace that she felt but didn't allow to breach the surface of her perfected face. She bowed her head and let them come to her. She let each one touch her and praise her and was grateful she couldn't puke in Heaven. Elicia just stood watching with the same hideous smile she had worn as she delivered her smiting from God.

By the time her groupies had finished groping her, the sun in Heaven was beginning to set. She bowed again and said, "My sheep," she knew now she should be saying *lamb* but decided that *sheep* fit better. "I must go home to my parents now. They are waiting for me. Stay sparkly," she shot her finger guns at her small adoring crowd as she had done before, but this time she threw in a wink and a big cheesy smile for good measure. Stripper to deified televangelist was quite the fall in her opinion. Too bad there was no money in Heaven, or Kat would be jetting around in her own private plane and drowning in cocaine and hookers. Kat doubted any of those toothy grinned holier than thou grifters were in Hell though. If she were given the chance, she would personally drag their greedy asses down there. Kat wanted a drink. Or ten.

She began to walk slowly toward her house. The sunset was a watercolor of pale amber bleeding into deep rose as the night sky slowly closed in on the sun. Kat thought it was utterly vile. Then the sun was gone, and the stars twinkled like the lights in the eyes of a soccer mom on amateur night at the strip club. The moon played bouncer, ready to bust the skulls of anyone who dared to spoil the night's beauty with the truth behind its fragile facade.

She could hear her parents laughing behind the front door as she put her hand on the knob and drew a deep breath. She didn't bother to knock, thinking that they would be expecting her. Her mother was, but her father wasn't. The look on his face as she walked into her new and possibly forever home told her he was as disappointed as she was. She searched his face for some sign that maybe there was another note from Satan, or Amon, or anyone at all not from this realm. She found nothing except her own sorrow reflected back to her.

Her mother, however, practically jumped from her place on the sofa, nearly toppling the monopoly board that had taken the place of her father's bottle of booze on the coffee table. It was a biblical version of the game, Kat noticed. Because of course it was. Kat very much preferred booze but knew that soon she would be sitting down to join the game.

Her mother embraced her, and Kat melted into her arms. She had been ready to abandon her mother for the rest of eternity, but now she accepted the hug and was grateful for it. Her mother let her go with a kiss on her cheek.

"What would you like for dinner?" her mother asked. "I can *make* anything you want," she beamed at her own joke. Kat's heart leapt as the *mom-joke* brought back memories of her childhood. But what she wanted was overcooked chicken and lumpy mashed potatoes. And perhaps a slightly mealy apple for dessert or an overcooked piece of pumpkin pie.

The look of joy on her mother's face stopped the thought in its tracks, so she said, "Do you remember how you used to make chicken and dumplings when it was raining outside?"

"Oh, I do, Kathryn. I do." Her smile turned into slight frown, "It's not raining though."

The sentence was barely out of her mouth when the sound of gently rolling thunder followed by the sound of the light tapping of rain drops on the roof. Her mother's frown melted, and a pot of chicken and dumplings appeared on the little dining room table. Kat smiled in spite of herself.

"Well," Kat said, "let's eat."

"Then we can play monopoly and read a bible verse before bed," her mother said, planting a kiss on the top of her head.

"Don't push it Louise," her father said. Her mother gave him a sheepish look, and then a smile.

They sat down to eat. The chicken and dumplings were exactly as she remembered. She wanted to hate it. To hate all of this, but at that moment she enjoyed it. She could hate everything later. As she forked mouthful after mouthful of tender chicken and fluffy dumplings into her mouth, she decided that if she were going to be stuck here, she would at least enjoy what she could, while she could. And for now, it was a nostalgic meal with her dead parents. She knew that there would be much frustration to come with whatever plan God had for her. He was going to exploit her for His own gain. She still hoped that Satan would try and come for her, but she wasn't holding her breath. Mostly because she didn't have any lungs.

After dinner, they did in fact sit down to play biblical monopoly. It was an odd version for sure, and she had little doubt that it was designed by God. The high-priced properties were church owned and tax exempt. And once you owned a set, you were issued an unlimited get out of jail free card. As the slums were plagued by endless fees, fines, taxes almost guaranteeing that once one found themselves in such a position as to be beholden to the church, poverty was inescapable but supposedly mitigated by the promise of paradise when you died. Picking oneself up by the bootstraps was encouraged, although the bootstraps almost consistently broke if tugged on too hard.

Kat found it hard to focus on the game, as she couldn't keep her mind off of Satan, Hell, and Amon. Thoughts of her lover brought feelings of heartbreak and lust. She found that she could be horny in Heaven even without her naughty bits, but the spark ended in nothing. A snapped live wire with wasted energy dripping out the broken end. Yet another heavenly insult.

Finally, the game ended, and Kat was able to say her goodnights and head to her revolting room. There wasn't much point in undressing, and she found her body here distressing anyway. A cruel joke it was. She closed her eyes and considered her plight. Satan's note said to hang tight. But she didn't know what that really meant. Her friends were gone, and she was this strange celebrity now in Heaven. Jess had said not to worry about getting sent to earth and being publicly excocted. Kat tried to remember the conversation. *Something about a toast in a dog's ass?* But that didn't seem to make sense. She had finally found friends in Heaven, only to watch them escape without her.

She tried wishing for a bottle of bourbon, and one appeared. But when she took a sip, she found it was dark sweet tea. She spit it out and caught herself before she screamed. No pot. No booze, or sex. Not even any books. Kat hung her head on her purple bed, but her gaze fell to the name *Kathy* spelled in extra glitter on her nipple less breasts. The anger boiled over then evaporated to pure sorrow. She grasped for any kind of hope. She tried wishing for a music player. Maybe Satan would figure out a way to put a message on it. And one appeared.

Kat's hands flew to her mouth. She picked up the player and put the headphones on. It didn't have any buttons other than play and stop. She pressed play. Church hymns began to play. She didn't recognize any of them although she was sure she had probably heard them at some point as a kid struggling to stay still on a hard wooden pew. She gritted her teeth and listened. Satan had come through in rock music, or what some might refer to as rock music. Not Kat, but someone. She flipped the player over and over, checking every inch for a backwards button. She found nothing. Finally, she gave up and chucked the thing across the room. It made a crash but didn't break.

"Kathryn?" Her mother called.

"I'm ok, uh…just..uh…dropped my bible," she cringed at the ridiculously dumb thing to say. Like her mother would believe she was reading the Bible.

"Oh, I'm so happy you're finally reading it, but you should be more careful with the word of God." Kat cringed again. Her mother was really buying the whole redeemed thing. Kat fell back on her bed and closed her eyes. She willed herself to sleep, the only real relief she had available to her in Heaven. She could still hear the soft raindrops landing on the roof. She tried to imagine it was blood, hoping she might dream of Hell.

She awoke to a perfect sun and a perfect morning. She didn't dream at all but was grateful anyway for the apparent unconsciousness. She sat up and blinked the non-existent sleepiness from her eyes. As her bare feet touched the floor, she thought about going to the bathroom. But then couldn't find a reason to. Her hair was perfect, she didn't need to pee or brush her teeth. She padded quietly down the hall and into the living room. She saw her parents sitting together on the sofa. They hadn't noticed her yet. Her mother was tucked into her father's arms. He had a book open, and they were both reading silently together. Her father wore a smile, they both did in fact. And Kat's heart swelled. As much as she hated Heaven and everything about it, she couldn't hate that. She stepped into the living room and broke the spell.

"Good morning, Kat," her father said.

"Morning Dad, Mom," she smiled back. "Did you remember to set the coffee pot?"

"Oh of course dear," her mother said and giggled. A cup of coffee appeared in Kat's hand. She took a sip and hid her resentment of its perfection behind a smile.

"I think I'm going to head to the Administration and see how my martyrdom is coming along." Kat figured she didn't have anything better to do. And the more she thought about it, the more curious she was about the dog butt toast thing. She intended to ask God himself. As hard as she tried, she couldn't think of any way He could make it much worse for her. And besides, she deserved to know.

"How exciting!" Her mother said over her own cup of coffee. "Your father has promised to take me to see Jesus speak."

"Oh, that's so nice mom." Her father rolled his eyes at her behind her mother's head, but the smile on his face told her he wasn't as annoyed as he was trying to look.

Kat waved goodbye as she stepped out into the daylight. There was no sign of the rain the night before. Except maybe the birds and squirrels were livelier. She wondered what they would eat if all the bird seed was gone. Maybe nothing at all. If that were the case, then maybe the shit covered fruit would eventually go back to normal. She saw one of them, hoping on the ground pecking at some grass. Kat walked toward the

Administration building, but tried to stay off the roads, hoping to avoid seeing any of her fans, or perhaps they should be called followers. She was creeped out, either way.

The path she walked took her through trees and shrubs. Occasionally, she brushed against leaves or other foliage, but it was soft as butter. Nothing scratched or caught on her robe, and there were no sticks or sharp rocks under her feet. She looked at the heavenly squirrels. Cute and soft looking and lacking the pointy teeth and claws of their counterparts in Hell. She heard a soft rustling coming from one of the trees. She stopped to look up. Expecting, maybe hoping to catch a new heavenly creature. And she was not disappointed. Although, she had been expecting whatever it was to have fur. This creature did not. It had scales.

A long fat snake, or serpent maybe, wound itself down the skinny trunk, and soon it was face to face with her. It looked like it could have been smiling as its forked tongue slipped out of its mouth and tickled her nose.

19

Kat watched as the snake wound its way around the tree trunk to the ground, then began to slither upright on its body. It balanced on its pointy tail and stood nearly ten feet tall, but only briefly, the snake began to fatten out and grow shorter. Its tail split and began to form legs and feet, Kat had to struggle to keep watching as the reptile face began to morph into something more human-ish. She had gotten used to Satan's ugly face, in fact, she didn't really find him all that ugly anymore. Kind of cute actually. Personality went a long way, she supposed. She waited to see his face now as the snake changed, but she didn't recognize it. Then she did, but it wasn't Satan. Soon Lyla stood in front of her.

Kat threw her arms around her one-time nemesis, although she was a bit bummed that it wasn't Satan. Lyla hugged her back, then her hands drifted down to her ass and the former mean-girl angel cupped her cheeks and squeezed. Kat released her grip, and Lyla did the same but planted a wet kiss on her cheek before disengaging.

"Wow, girl…you look awful," Lyla said. Looking as she had in Heaven.

"Right? You too. You look like a starving supermodel."

Lyla laughed, "I feel a little weird too. But Satan, and I, frankly, thought that I would be the best one to get you out of here. We're going to try and barter with God."

"Wait a barter? Lyla, I won't let you sacrifice your place in Hell,"

"Oh no worries. I wouldn't do that. I've done a lot of work on myself in Hell, but trust me I'm not that selfless," she giggled. "But you dragged me down once, I'll just come with you when he sends you down."

"How do you know that will work? And how did you even get here now? Maybe I can just leave with you the way you came in?"

"No, the small hole closed as I came in. Satan transformed me just so I can slip through, but it's closed now. It wasn't quite a portal, our physics team said those are not going to be a thing anymore. God fixed that glitch permanently. But Satan was once God's special angel, as I was and so he was able to manipulate a small opening for me. But only a very narrow thing. Hence the snake body."

"I guess that makes sense, but why a snake? He could have picked something even smaller."

"He thought it would be funny," Lyla laughed again. "You know the whole Adam and Eve thing and talking snake.'

"Of course," and Kat felt silly for not getting the joke right away, but she was raised Catholic, and the bible stories weren't really her thing. "So how do we tell God you got here though?"

"Easy, we just tell him that Satan sent me back because he wants to trade me for you. I'll play the goody two shoes role like I was before. A desperate sycophant begging for help. God loves begging."

"Yeah, but that doesn't mean He'll actually grant you anything. And what if you get stuck here like me? Lyla, I dig Satan and all, but that guy isn't all that great at planning stuff."

"He said something about a backup plan. He didn't say much, but it sounded like a last resort kind of thing. He also didn't say much about the little rip he made for me, but I watched him do it and it didn't look easy. He got so pale he was almost pink," she paused for a moment. "Not that it matters much, but I think he started wearing make-up. What is that all about?"

Kat thought she knew actually, but it was only supposition so she said, "I couldn't say. Maybe he's just trying a new look?"

"That makes sense, I guess. Ok, so are you ready to talk to the big man?" Lyla said. "I'm already getting anxious to get back to Hell."

"Hang on. I have a few questions first," Kat had around a million questions, but she was only going to ask a few. "Did Alice and Jess make it down? How many others got through?"

Lyla smacked her forehead, "Oh, I'm sorry. I was in such a big ass hurry I forgot all about them. Ok, so yes, they made it back along with a butt ton of others. It created a bit of a back log at the intake actually. Mostly because Satan wants to greet each one personally. The logistics are a bit tricky too. A bunch of them brought their dogs. But Satan is pleased as punch to have them. He's got his minions helping to get everyone settled." Lyla took a breath, "Oh and Amon and Lucifer said to say Hi, Buster didn't say anything." She laughed.

That news made Kat happy, but she still wasn't sold on the whole fake barter thing with God. She wondered if maybe it would be easier to try and strike a deal with Jesus instead. He was much less scary at least. But she wasn't sure if he had the power to send her home.

"Hey, so what if we try to barter with Jesus instead? I think he'd be easier to work with," Kat asked. Lyla was starting to look anxious.

"I knew Jesus about as well as anyone could when I was here. It was how I gained such favor with God, and I don't think he actually has any kind of power."

Kat thought she was right, but pressed anyway, if only to avoid a confrontation with God, "Wasn't he in charge of salvation and all that though? Like isn't he the one who sends people to Hell for not believing in the blood sacrifice thing?"

"That was the story, yes. But I don't think Jesus was ever really on earth in the first place Kat. It was just a fairytale. I mean look at the pictures and paintings of him. He's a white dude, from the middle east. An image created by people who took vague text and conjured up a face that fit what they needed it to." Lyla was starting to shift from one foot to the other, obviously growing impatient. "Then they started to see that face all over the place. People are good at seeing faces where there aren't any. Like clouds or drywall."

"Or toast or a dog's ass," Kat mused.

"Um…sure," Lyla looked confused. "But yeah. Let's go. This place is making me uneasy."

Kat shrugged. She didn't think this was a good idea at all. But didn't know what else to do. She motioned for Lyla to follow her, and they began to walk through the trees toward the administration building. They stayed on the path that Kat had already been on. Neither one wanted to be recognized. Kat tried to stay positive as they exited the forest, but it was tough. The big building looked extra sparkly as they approached the steps.

Kat was about to open the doors when a loud noise boiled up behind her. She turned to look, and a mob of angels had appeared from apparently nowhere. Heading the pack was Elicia. Kat rolled her eyes, as she faced the crowd and bowed. The crowd swooned as one.

"Kathy, spare a few minutes for your admirers?" Elicia said with a nasty gleam in her eye.

Kat said, "No time, I have important business with God to attend to."

She grasped the handle of the large door and pulled it open, ushering Lyla through first as she shot the crowd with her finger guns and graced them with her new catch phrase, "Stay sparkly!"

Kat hadn't been inside the admin building since she had been back. The large obnoxious décor hadn't changed. Done in gold and deep red, she thought it looked like a brothel's attempt to look classy. She saw that Chad (or was it, Chris?) was still at the counter. He looked at her and she saw recognition, then contempt flash briefly through his eyes. She smiled, winked, and pointed a finger gun at him. Lyla giggled next to her.

As they approached the counter, Chad said, "Lyla? Is that you?"

"It is," Lyla put on her mean girl smile. Kat was almost alarmed at how easily it came back to her. "We need to speak to God, please."

Chad looked at Kat suspiciously, "I know you are supposed to be the new savior, Kathy. But you'll always be a whore to me."

"Not a whore. A slut. Thank you very much," Kat smiled again.

"The only reason she's not a whore is because she died before she had the chance to charge for it," Lyla sneered. "Satan couldn't keep me from my place here in Heaven, and I snuck back in. But there are a few loose ends we need to clear up with the big Guy. He's expecting us."

"He is?" Chad asked suspiciously, directing his intense unbroken gaze at Kat.

"He is," Lyla said firmly. "No more dicking around, I demand to speak with God this instant." Chad recoiled, but as Lyla glared at him, he was forced to move his stare from Kat to Lyla. She didn't flinch.

The hallway on the right lit up and Chad motioned for them to proceed. Lyla didn't break her eye contact with him as they made their way toward the long hallway that led to

God. There was only one door at the end. It opened as they neared it.

A booming voice could be heard coming from the open door, and Kat was glad she didn't have any bowels, "Come in my children."

Lyla held her head high, floating on a confidence that Kat didn't feel at all. Kat wanted to run in the other direction. But she moved forward anyway. God looked as she remembered, a bearded old man in a white robe sitting on a throne made of clouds. And Kat had thought that Satan's look was cliché.

Lyla bent down on one knee, "My lord. I come to you humbled by hellfire."

Now that's how you talk to a deity, Kat thought. She tried to mimic her friend.

Kat bent down and said, "My lord, I come to you…um humbled by your donuts." *Ok, so it needs some work.*

"One of my finest creations," He said. Kat wasn't sure if He meant her or the donuts but decided it didn't matter. "Kathy, you know now that I have a divine plan for you. You are to be the next savior."

Lyla stood up, so Kat did the same, "Yeah about that…."

Lyla interrupted, "Satan has sent me back in an effort to trade my soul for Kat's. But I will not be manipulated by the father of lies. I am at your disposal dear Lord; my soul is forever devoted to you and your divine plan." Kat cocked her head, but figured that Lyla had a plan.

"My child, you have suffered enough. Go forth and enjoy the place in Heaven you have earned. When it comes time for the crucifixion, you will have a front seat."

"Wait what?" Kat said, as Lyla bowed and left the room. Kat watched her leave, confused. Kat was still trying to figure out what had just happened. Had her friend just delivered her to a malignant deity?

"In ten days, you will be put on the cross to die. You will be entombed for three days, then resurrected as savior."

"You're sending me to earth?"

"No. You are not worthy of such a mission. Nor can you be trusted. The people of Heaven have been misled to believe that they can thwart my authority. Your disobedience has spread and led my sheep out of the paradise I have made for them. Your sacrifice will absolve the sins of those who weren't able to leave through your gaping hole. Those souls who desired to leave, but couldn't, will only be able to enjoy the things in Heaven that have my approval. I know about the donuts of knowledge you have used with the help of Satan to corrupt my subjects. They are sinners again, and your blood will wash away their sins."

Kat had to stifle a laugh at *gaping hole*, but fear and then realization hit her, "So you're going to punish everyone who saw through your bullshit but couldn't leave? Now that you can't punish them with Hell, you're going to punish them with Christian rock and bland literature?"

Kat had to admit it was utterly diabolical. Satan could learn a few things from God about eternal punishment. Your skin grows back, but a Stryper song lives in your brain forever. Pure evil.

"The fault lies with you, Kathy." God scowled at her, but she was too angry to be scared.

"You aren't actually able to send anyone to earth, are you?"

God's face flushed with anger, "Who are you to question my abilities?" The squishy clouds around her trembled with His voice and the light flickered.

"Apparently the one who doesn't buy your bullshit. Go ahead and do your worst," she said and regretted it in an instant. A white flame began at her bare feet and made its way up her body, to her mouth which hung open as the pain took her voice before the flames could reach her face. Soon she was reduced to a pillar of salt. Only her eyeballs remained, she blinked as she wished she could say, but could only think as her mouth was gone, *a pillar of salt, how fucking predictable.* Then there were no more thoughts.

20

Kat awoke in her hideous bed. She could hear her parents talking in the living room but couldn't make out what they were saying. Her body was intact again, except for the good parts of course. The memory of the pain of her meeting with God burned brightly in her mind. She tried to stuff it back into the recesses of her mind, but each time it resurfaced she relived the agony again. It was as if each nerve was on fire at the same time and she couldn't stop herself from feeling it again and again as she laid there. She had seen some stuff in Hell that looked like it hurt, but she didn't think even Satan was capable of inflicting the kind of pain she had felt when God turned her to salt. *What a dick,* she shuddered.

The physical pain was bad, but Lyla's betrayal was worse. Like way worse. Kat found it hard to believe. Lyla had been her friend. Her slutty pan sexual polyamorous friend. She didn't understand how she could have misjudged her so badly. It seemed that she had just been biding her time in Hell to exact her revenge. Kat had to think that was the case. That she was putting on a show until she had a chance to get back to Heaven to resume licking God's balls. If so, Kat thought she had earned herself an Oscar. No, she had earned herself like three Oscars. A real Meryl fucking Streep.

As much as she hated the bed she was lying in, she found she didn't want to get out of it. She didn't want to face what was ahead of her. She didn't doubt for a second that God was going to keep His word. She would be tortured and executed, and she would feel every bit of it. She was going to be martyred. Fake martyred, but still. She had thought that Satan had come for her in the form of a snake, but it was Lyla coming to betray her. She wondered if Satan even knew what had happened. Did he even really send her, or did she just slither her way into Heaven on her own? Kat wanted to die. For good. But she had tried that already, and it hadn't worked. And she was about to die again, apparently just for the amusement of a blood thirsty deity.

Kat closed her eyes and tried to sleep, but it wouldn't come. And the harder she tried to keep her mind off of the encounter with God, the more the memory came, bringing the pain with it. She clenched her teeth, trying to stay silent, but failed.

"Kathryn?" Her mother called through the closed door.

"It's ok mom."

Her mother opened the door and stepped into the room. She was holding a light pink washcloth. Her mom propped the pillows up behind her head, so she could sit up slightly. She held the cool damp cloth to her forehead. Kat wanted to cry. Again.

"Here, maybe this will help. The suffering you're enduring is all part of your sacrifice Kat. You have been chosen to save souls, and I'm so proud of you."

Kat closed her eyes. Trying to control her thoughts and memories so to avoid another reliving of being reduced to a pile of salt. She could smell her mother's perfume as she sat next to her on the bed. Comforting her daughter from the holy bullshit of the deity she had devoted her life to worshipping. Kat was becoming angry. She knew that her parents were happy here now in Heaven, and she wanted to let them enjoy it. Even if that meant separating forever, however she was unable to bite her tongue any longer about her true feelings.

"Mom, if God can do anything, why does He make people suffer? Why doesn't He just make everything ok?"

"He works in mysterious ways Kathryn, we are not to question them," her mother's tone had darkened. "I know now that you caused all sorts of trouble and were sent to Hell. God has granted you another chance. That proves that He is good. You should be grateful for His mercy, and the chance to save others."

"Save them from what though? He is doing this to me to save the souls that are already here. That doesn't make sense mom."

"We don't question God."

"But why?"

"Because He could punish us," her voice had grown tiny now.

"Punish us for using the minds He supposedly created for us? According to the bible, He created evil and Hell. He could just get rid of evil, and no one would be able to sin and go to Hell. But instead, we are born in sin? Doomed unless we repent for the way we were born? Nothing about that strikes you as fu…uh messed up?"

"I don't think you're thinking clearly, you should rest. Your big day is tomorrow. This will all be over soon."

Kat opened her eyes and looked into her mother's, as she did, the memory of the pain came flooding into her mind. Her back arched and she screamed. Her mother left the room. As her nerve endings calmed down, she realized that it hadn't been as bad as it had the time before. She wondered if she was getting used to it, or if it was losing its intensity. She deliberately brought on the pain. It came, and it sucked, but it was getting easier each time.

Kat took a pillow from behind her head and bit down on it hard as she brought back the memory of what God had done to her. Then she did it again. And again. And each time, it got easier. Soon she didn't need the pillow. She found that she no longer feared the pain. Mostly because it had been reduced to the level of just about nothing. A dull ache, and even that was waning. She smirked and got out of bed. She might not have won the war, but she had won at least one small battle. She was ready to win another. Even if she had to do it alone. She smoothed her robe and her hair although neither required it. She opened the door to her room.

Her parents weren't in the living room as she had thought they would be. She opened the front door and found them sitting on the porch bench watching the animals play in the trees and grass. Her mother rested her head on her father's shoulder. The look of contentment she had seen earlier had been replaced by melancholy. She had tried to bring some logic to her mother and had instead made her upset.

"Hey mom, it's ok now. The pain is just about gone. I'm going for walk to clear my head, and get ready for tomorrow," she turned up the corners of her mouth in what she hoped looked like a smile.

Her parents waved at her as she walked down the little path and through the gate. She wasn't sure where she was going to go. The day was bright, and sparkly and it hurt her eyes. She resented every bit of the light. Kat spotted some angels and decided she didn't want anything to do with them and slipped into the trees and off of the street. She found herself in the same spot where Lyla had snuck her way back into Heaven. She wondered if maybe Lyla had been lying about the hole being closed. The more she thought about it, the more likely that seemed.

She found the tree and looked up into the leaves. There were no animals playing in it and she thought that was a good sign. The two places the portals had been didn't have any wildlife either. Kat began to climb. She sat on the branch where she had seen Lyla first and put her hands on the smooth bark hoping to feel a break or tear or something to indicate where a hole could be. She found nothing and decided to move a bit farther up to the next branch. This one was a bit flimsier, and she felt it sway under her weight. Again, she felt all the way around the trunk and the branch. This time she was rewarded with a slight anomaly in the bark. A little indent. Kat stuck her finger in it.

Her finger went in only a little of the way and she couldn't tell if it was just an indent or an actual hole. She pushed farther and watched her fingernail disappear. She held her breath as the excitement washed over her. She pushed her finger in deeper, hoping to widen the hole. It stayed the same size. She wondered how in the hell a snake could've fit through the damned thing at all. The only part she could think that would fit would be its tongue. Kat bent her head down and stuck her tongue in the hole. She thought she could taste sulfur on the other side. Or brimstone maybe. She waggled it back and forth, tasting.

Something bit her. Then chattered. A hell squirrel. She withdrew her tongue but put her lips around the hole and blew. She heard more chattering. She whispered through the hole, thinking maybe something or someone might hear her. "Hey, is anyone there?" She was rewarded with more chattering. She put her nose in and drew in deeply. She thought she could smell the lake of fire. She couldn't be sure. And even if it was, she probably wouldn't find anyone there anyway. The lake of fire was kind of cool, but not much of a tourist destination. She stuck her finger back in the hole but found her finger didn't go as far in as it had at first. She pushed harder, thinking maybe she could stretch it. But it wouldn't budge.

She pulled out her finger, and as she did, she watched the hole go from hole to indent and finally to nothing. Lyla had told the truth. The hole was closed. It just hadn't closed immediately. Not much of a consolation, given her utter betrayal and the lie she had told. Kat felt really stupid for believing she had changed from who she had been in Heaven. She was still the nasty mean girl she had been. Lyla had only gotten better at it. Kat hopped down from the tree. The ground seemed to catch her and absorbed the shock as she landed. She had expected it to hurt now that pain seemed to be a thing in Heaven.

She kept walking, even more unsure about where she was going than before. She came to a road on the other side of the dense trees she had been navigating. She saw she was close to a small little park. It was empty and she was grateful. Well mostly empty. She saw Jesus sitting on one side of a teeter toter. The end of the board where he sat was on the ground. He looked sad. Kat didn't want to care. She wondered why she did. But she did. She went over to him and put a soft hand on his shoulder.

"God doesn't want me anymore," said the dejected half deity.

"Oh no, that's not true," Kat had no clue if she were lying or not.

"You're going to be the new savior."

"Meh, it's just a stunt. You'll be more popular than the Beatles again in no time. Trust me, I'll be forgotten."

"The Beatles?"

"Biggest band ever, they tried to say they were bigger than you on earth but faced a major clap back," She wasn't sure this was true at all, but thought it sounded good. "Trust me, you're still cool down there. And I'm just a flash in the pan here. In fact, once people see how terrible a martyr I am, you'll be even more loved."

"You think so?"

Kat nodded her head because she actually did. She wasn't cut out for this. And the whole thing was performative. A crucifixion for shits and giggles. Especially if she weren't actually going to go to earth. God would get His spin on her story, and she could spend the rest of eternity in pious misery.

Jesus perked up and smiled, "Well in that case, would you like to wash my feet?"

Kat cringed and shook her head no. She turned in the direction of her parents' home. The sun was starting to set, and she thought she might as well get back and wait for the day to come. At the very least, she would be happy to have this whole mess over with. She hoped she was right that she would just fade into obscurity. Maybe God would grant her booze again. Or another cat. That thought brought an intense sadness as she thought of Buster and Lucifer. And then there was Amon and Satan and her friends.

As she got closer to her house, Kat noticed someone was following her. She turned to see an angel following her, soon another joined that one. Then another ten. Soon it was a hundred. By the time she reached her front door, there were thousands.

21

Kat hurried inside and slammed the door. The crowd that had gathered outside was huge but silent. Which was about as creepy as is could get. Until they all lit candles, then it got even creepier. The view from the kitchen window wasn't a lake of fire but a sea of tiny white lights. The dazzling sight burned her eyes, but when she closed them, the light shredded her eyelids anyway.

Her parents sat in the living room on the sofa. Beelzebub laid at her father's feet, snoring lightly. They looked at her but only her mother smiled. A weak smile that lacked any kind of warmth. Kat only nodded and went past them to her room. She threw herself on her bed and sighed. A moment later her father walked in. He didn't knock. There wasn't much of a point.

"This is stupid," he said.

Kat sat up and rolled her eyes, "Yeah, it's pretty stupid. But hey, I might show up in a dog's asshole on earth. So, there's that."

Her father frowned at her, "Um?"

"Meh… it doesn't matter. I feel like kind of an ass though. I'm happy that I helped to get people out, but I fucked it up for a bunch more, I think. He knew about the donuts and everyone who didn't get out is going to be stuck living under God's thumb because of me. And I'm stuck here too. I messed up pretty bad Dad."

"You helped a lot of people. And you're kind of a badass in my book for that. The bravest soul I know. I bet this all blows over at some point when the big guy finds something else to amuse Him. It won't be so bad," he tried to put on a reassuring smile. "And it will be the last time you have to die…hopefully," his smile widened with encouragement. Kat giggled.

"I guess. I miss my friends and my cats."

"You'll have the others that at least know the truth and I'll bet they'll want to find other people that would rather be in Hell too. He knew about the donuts, but I don't think he's caught on to the shitty fruit. No one's eating it anymore. The donuts of knowledge are gone, but at least you have stopped the ignorance from spreading."

"I almost forgot about that. Ha! That makes me feel a bit better," Kat hugged him.

"Maybe one day, there'll be another portal or something. Eternity is a long time, and things change. Even in Heaven. The only guarantee we ever have, is impermanence."

Kat knew he was right, but it was still bittersweet. He kissed her forehead, and she laid back down. She was glad that her mother hadn't come in to try and make her feel better. She hadn't made her feel better since she was a kid. Since she died the first time at least, nothing had fucked her up quite as having to face the feelings she had about her mother. She loved her of course, and she knew that her mother loved her back. But it was hard to accept her blind faith toward a being that, at least to Kat, simply seemed motivated by His own ego. He wasn't omniscient, omnipotent, and definitely not benevolent. God's grace is nothing but an illusion of His own creation. He hadn't sent His son to earth, only dropped him into a story. He was only a façade held together by the fear of a Hell that people didn't understand. A deity composed entirely of misinformation and myth.

But her father was right, and even if he weren't, she didn't see much recourse now. Her allies were gone, and her fate was sealed. Kat had to cling to the hope that things would blow over, eternity was a long-damned time. Kat tried to wish herself to sleep but sleep, like orgasms were impossible. Part of her martyrdom she figured. After this crap was over, she would probably be granted sleep again. Maybe she could even just sleep away eternity. The thought actually brought some comfort. Rather than being bored and frustrated forever, she could just not wake up. It's what she had thought was going to happen when she closed her eyes for the last time on earth.

But in the meantime, she had a whole night to kill. She didn't want to read the bible, which was all of her books except for the book on manners, so she plucked it off the shelf and opened it.

It was not the book of manners. Kat smiled. The title page looked like it was, but past that there were paintings. Jess paintings. Each page held a picture. Some were animals, mostly cats. Some abstract. None of them were like the paintings she had seen strewn around her easel when she had first come upon her fresh out of the portal. These were imperfect. A perfect reflection of humanity. Kat knew they had been painted in Hell. She must have slipped it in with the music player and the note from Satan.

The last page held a handwritten note:

Kat, you have brought me and so many others so much joy. Know that you are my hero and my friend. Please look at these and remember me. And maybe one day we'll meet again in Hell.

-J

Kat held the book close to her chest. Her eyes felt like they were going to burst. She returned to the first page and went through each picture again slowly. Relishing each one. Trying to memorize each of them in case God took this from her too. If there was anything that she had learned it was not to take any pleasure, no matter how small or seemingly insignificant, for granted. Even in death, joy is precious because sorrow could be lurking around the corner. At that moment, Jess' art was pure joy. The kind of joy that Heaven had promised but could never deliver.

Reluctantly, Kat put the book back on the shelf. She didn't think that God was watching her, but if He were, He might wonder why she was smiling into a book of manners. She was restless though. She closed her eyes one more time in an attempt to pass the time with sleep. She tried to still her mind and breathe. Sort of. When she opened her eyes again, she saw light creeping in through her window. The sun was coming up.

Kat slid off her bed and padded into her pointless bathroom. She wasn't sure when or how this would all play out. She sure as hell wasn't going to make it easy by walking to the execution site herself. She looked at the big luxurious bathtub, exactly like the kind she had always wanted on earth. She drew a bath and slipped out of her robe and into the perfectly warm water. Practicing her new perspective of enjoying what she could when she could. She leaned her head back and closed her eyes again.

Only a split second later she opened them to the sound of the crowd outside making noise. It sounded angry, which surprised her. Kat couldn't understand why they would be angry at the person who was going to save them...again. But they sounded agitated. Kat thought they must simply be riled up by the sheer blood lust of the God they believed had saved them from the eternal punishment He himself had created. Or maybe they were upset that God was putting her through this pointless PR stunt. She had really hoped that by introducing the donuts of knowledge that at least some of the souls in Heaven would begin to see that God was not just an asshole but a sadist too.

As she listened to the crowd, she sunk lower into the water, which had surprisingly gone cold. Probably because God wanted her to face her fate. She slunk lower into the increasingly chilly water out of sheer spite. The warm water had felt good, defiance felt better. Her mother walked in, and she dunked her whole head under.

"It's time," her mother said. Her voice sounded muffled.

Kat stayed underwater. *Ha! I have no lungs, nana nana boo boo stick your head in doo doo.* The old kid's rhyme played in her head without her specifically remembering it. Suddenly the tub was empty and dry. So was Kat. Her body was dry, and her heart empty.

"Fine," and she rose up out of the tub. As she stood up, a golden robe draped around her pleasureless body. It sparkled something fierce, but at least her name or her name-ish, wasn't on the front anymore. She was still trying to practice gratitude for the little things. Her mother took her hand and led her to the front door, saying nothing. Her father had a somber look on his face as he watched her put her hand on the door.

Before Kat could turn the knob, he embraced her and whispered in her ear, "It's all going to be okay Kat. I promise."

She wished she could believe him, but that was only another wish that wouldn't be granted in Heaven. She turned the knob to greet the mob outside that awaited her. Elicia was right up in front holding upright a large wooden cross. It was covered in glitter because of course it was. It looked as if she had spread glue on the thing and sprinkled it herself. A monstrous smile sat high above her enormous jugs. Kat had only a moment to wonder if she had nipples before the cross was thrust upon her. She put her hands out quickly to catch it before it landed on her parents' front door.

"Kathryn, can I help you carry it?" Her mother asked.

"No, it's fine," Kat said as the weight of it bared down on her.

Kat took the cross on her back as the crowd parted to let her through to her extra death. A bonus death. The cross wasn't all that heavy, but the burden was overwhelming anyway. Elicia was following right behind her and relished her struggles.

"That is the weight of the sin you have brought to Heaven…Kathy."

If Kat could have swung the glittery torture device like a baseball bat, she would have gleefully done so. The other angels in the horde seemed to sneer along with their leader. Kat realized that what she had heard as anger while she took her short bath, was actually more like anticipation. The angels that had gathered weren't the ones who had discovered the truth, the ones she was meant to re-save, but the ones that were rooting for her misery. She had thought that Lyla and the other shithead angels were anomalies. A bunch of assholes in an otherwise compassionate population of dead people. But there were now thousands, maybe hundreds of thousands of these shitheads now. It was like a Grateful Dead show for fuck wads instead of stoners. They had been lining up wanting to touch her and she had thought she was some sort of celebrity, but no. She was just main attraction in this fucked up horror movie.

There hadn't been any fatigue or soreness in Heaven. Before God decided to make her a martyr, she hadn't felt any pain, but she felt all of it now. It drowned her lust for defiance. She moved her hand to get a better grip and felt a large splinter pierce her skin.

"Owww!"

Elicia giggled and the angel horde giggled with her.

Mercifully, Kat came upon the platform where Jesus liked to speak. He stood upon it completely devoid of the melancholy he had worn when she had seen him last. He looked almost giddy. But trying to hide it. He was shifting from foot to foot holding a golden tablet in his hands. She guessed it was the sermon he was going to give as she was nailed to the cross. He kept trying to suppress his smile, but it wouldn't stay hidden. He looked like a kid on Christmas morning. Or maybe Easter.

The cross was taken from her. It stood on its own then. It had secured itself into the ground. Two hunky angels took each of her arms and began to lift her up. She noticed that they had wings. Not the little wings that she had seen when she had first gotten to Heaven. But large feathered ones. They were naked. And intact, although she didn't think they looked equipped for much more than writing their names in the snow. She looked at their tiny junk and smirked at them. The angels paid no attention as they lifted her up and set her feet on the little nub meant for her to stand on.

She knew what was coming next but was horrified anyway as they produced three unbelievably large nails. They floated on either side of her, waiting for instructions. A crown of thorns replaced her halo, and a trickle of blood ran into her eyes. She couldn't tell if it was sparkly or not, but thought it was safe to assume that it was. The two angels and the rest of the crowd turned their attention to Jesus who was no longer trying to hide his huge grin. Some were watching with excitement, but a larger portion had looks of terror and disgust. The latter portion she recognized hadn't been the ones outside her house. She knew that these were the ones she had enlightened. The ones that had seen the hypocrisy and vapidness of Heaven. Kat saw her parents behind the crowd. Her mother looked disturbed, and her father had his head down unable to watch.

Kat heard Jesus take a deep breath and watched him open his mouth to speak, but before he could, dark clouds appeared overhead.

22

Jesus looked up to the darkening sky. Kat and the rest of their audience followed his gaze up to the clouds. These weren't the gray bluish clouds of a fresh spring rain, which was the only kind of rain that came in Heaven. The clouds were so dark they were nearly black. So black, they completely obliterated the sun. A strange kind of artificial night fell over the land, mixed with an eerie silence. For the first time since she had died, Kat couldn't see anything sparkle in Heaven. It was as if the light of Heaven itself had been snuffed out.

Kat could feel something in the air, a latent rumbling. Something bubbling up. She closed her eyes and waited for God to come and make His appearance. Coming to show His might. Simply being nailed to a cross wasn't going to be good enough. She braced herself in anticipation of the pain of another smiting almost wishing he had just stuck with the nails. *And here I thought I was finally going to get nailed in Heaven,* her panicked brain thought. A terrible silence hung heavy as she and everyone else waited for God's wrath.

A loud ripping noise broke the spell. A sound like the tearing of a strong fabric, like the ass of a pair of work jeans separating at the seam. Nostalgic fart giggles tore through the silence, until the source of the sound became clear. The tip of a blade sliced the black clouds, ripping the sky downward. Red fire and smoke bled through the fresh cut in the sky. All remaining giggles ceased.

The crowd watched in horror while Kat watched with glee, as a tiny round winged black and white cat flew valiantly through the hole in the sky. Lucifer wore only a little gold horned helmet, armor, and an expression of pure determination. Directly behind him flew Buster, who seemed to be riding on wings of pure rage and also the wings that Satan must have given him. *Amon must have forgotten to feed him....* Kat thought deliriously.

Kat only had a moment to smile at her little feline heroes, as another being tore through the rip. Kat had to look away as the white light burned her eyes. The most magnificent angel she had ever seen burst through the fabric of Heaven. The ground shook as he touched down on the ground next to the platform where Jesus stood trembling. Kat estimated that he must be at least seven feet tall. He was a being of almost pure light. Muscles rippled under a white robe, his face was unadulterated beauty, and on top of his head was a golden helmet from which a large penis stood erect. Satan. He looked up at her, made the sign of the devil horns with his hands, and stuck out his tongue. Kat knew then that her father had been right. Everything was going to be okay.

Lucifer and Buster touched down on the arms of the cross on either side of her head. The two angels who had lifted her up only a few moments ago each took a lunge at the cats. Buster swiped a claw and caught one of the angels on the cheek, drawing golden glittering blood. Not red, but gold, almost yellow. Kat registered the odd color but didn't have time to think much about it.

Lucifer drove his little helmet horn into the other angel's chest but only succeeded in poking him a little. Not to be deterred, Lucifer promptly turned around and flashed his butthole. The angel frowned and knocked Lucifer off the side of the cross. He screeched as he fell, but then remembered his wings and caught himself before he could fall to the ground. Kat was still balancing on the little perch made for her feet, she held on to both arms of the cross and kicked out one foot as hard as she could. It was perhaps her finest kick in all of her life or death and landed it squarely in the balls of the angel who had dared to hit her cat.

"You fucking monster," she cried as she felt her bare foot connect. The angel only smirked. "Figures they were just ornamental, not much of a show though. It's a bit drafty up here…so I get the shrinkage." The smirking angel punched her straight in the jaw and sent her tumbling to the ground, her robe flapping up around her waist, but not revealing much. She was embarrassed just the same given that she had just been making fun of the angel's junk, and she had no such junk of her own to make fun of. But her embarrassment fled when she hit the ground with a thud. Her head rang, and she knew that she would still feel pain in Heaven.

The two un-hung angels were on her in an instant. The one that Buster had scratched was still oozing that odd yellow blood. She was lying on her face. One of the angels pinned her legs while the other grabbed her by the back of her hair and slammed her face into the ground. The warm dirt that had welcomed and cushioned her bare feet, felt like asphalt in the parking lot of her old strip club. Her nose popped like an overripe tomato. Her eyes spilled tears. They didn't just fill up, and hot wet tears mixed with the blood running down her chin. She tried to scream, when she felt her head rise up against her will and slam back down. She thought that next time she made fun of a dude's junk she needed to make sure she had a bouncer around to back her up. Kat wondered then where Satan was. What he was doing while she was at the mercy of these horrendous angels. She tried to look up, but her vision was blurred. She laid perfectly still. Hoping that they would assume she was dead. Like really Heaven dead. And to her surprise it seemed to work. She felt the hand holding her hair depart along with the pressure on her legs.

Kat kept her face to the ground and stayed unmoving. She focused on the sounds around her. Screams and howls swarmed her ears, she couldn't tell whom they were coming from. A warm shower of thick liquid drenched her, but she stayed still. Terrified to attract the attention of more asshole angels. But when she heard a loud screech that sounded like Lucifer, she couldn't wait any longer to look up. But when she did, she didn't see her heaven turned hell cat.

The scene around her was exactly what she had imagined Hell to be when she was a little kid. Not the cartoon version, but the gore-soaked agony of tortured souls. Winged sword wielding demons lopped off the heads of warrior angels, their golden blood rained down from the sky. Pieces of giant feathery wings fell with yellow haired severed heads. She tried to find to Satan or her cats in the melee but failed. The crowd that had come to watch had fled, including her parents.

A wet splat came to her left and she saw with horror the face of the angel that Buster had scratched. His eyes stared off into nothing, she didn't know where his body had landed. Kat rolled away quickly. She found the golden blood to be only slightly less disturbing than the dark red of human blood. She stood up on wobbly legs. No one was paying much attention to her, and she was grateful for that. She hurt all over, but mostly her face. She stumbled toward the rip in the sky. It seemed an impossible distance. Demons poured through it, all ready to fight. She even saw a few hell rabbits and squirrels dashing through. She wasn't sure much good they would do, but she appreciated the effort. They were tough little fuckers.

She started to run toward the rip which had reached the ground and went all the way up into the sky. As she got closer, she saw that the flow of Hell's army was beginning to ebb. Then it stopped and began to reverse. The creatures and demons were going back through. Some of Heavens inhabitants followed them. The wound was beginning to heal. Heaven was repairing itself. She saw one of Satan's minions cut down as they tried to get back through, an angel grinned as it held the bloody sword. The minion's body caught fire and burned to ash in an instant.

Something hit Kat's shin and sent her sprawling on the ground. She heard Elicia laugh and felt a kick to her side. If the breath hadn't been knocked out of her, Kat was sure she would have had something snarky to say. It was on the tip of her tongue, she just had to think of it. Then Elicia squealed and Kat felt a strong hand pick her up. She was sure it was Satan, or possibly Amon, but when she turned to look, it was Lyla. *Why was it always Lyla?* Kat thought. Lyla was smiling and holding a red-haired scalp. Elicia lay in a pool of golden blood. Lyla was in her angel form, but Kat thought she was beautiful anyway.

"Come, it's time to get the hell out of here," Lyla said. Smiling at her own pun. Kat wanted to ask about her cats and Satan but didn't have time. Lyla took her into her arms and began to run. As she approached the closing gap, she hurled Kat through the to the other side.

Kat landed on the soft black sand of the beach at the lake of fire. She turned to look back into Heaven and saw Lyla fighting with yet another of God's own heavenly minions. Lyla didn't look like she was winning. The rip was closing quicker now, and she was about to go back through to help her friend, but Buster and Lucifer flew down and landed on the angel's back, biting and scratching, giving Lyla just enough time to bring the enormous sword she was holding down on her attacker's head, slicing clean through. The angel fell in two perfectly symmetrical pieces. She had to give her little Heaven cat credit. He hated Lyla even after she had made it to Hell. Lyla and her two hellcats rushed through into Hell and landed next to her on the sand.

"Where is Satan?" Kat asked, "Is he still in there?"

"I don't know," Lyla said breathlessly. She had come back to her form in Hell.

"We can't leave him there, did Amon come too? Oh fuck, what a mess. All those dead angels," Kat was still trying to process the whole situation.

"I'm here," Amon said from behind her. "Satan is still in there."

There was only a little sliver left of the opening into Heaven. Through it, Kat squinted her eyes in an effort to see Satan. Who she saw instead were her parents running for the opening her dad's dog following behind. Kat reached her hand through the hole and grasped her mother's hand. She yanked as hard as she could, and her mother, father, and Beelzebub slipped through as the hole closed with a loud pop.

The sky over the Lake of Fire turned a deep purple, deeper purple than it usually was. There was a loud crack of thunder, and the purple sky spit out a golden helmet that hit the edge of the lake. Kat ran over to pick it up before the liquid fire could destroy it. The penis on the top of it was limp. Kat began to cry.

She was back in Hell. Surrounded by her lover, her parents, her now ride or die bestie, and her two fearless felines with the knowledge that Satan, ruler of Hell had sacrificed himself to save her. Amon and Lyla hugged her while Buster and Lucifer clung to her legs both of them occasionally shooting a death stare at Beelzebub. They had lost their wings. When Amon and Lyla finally let go, she saw her parents locked in each other's arms.

Kat went to her mother, "Mom? Are you okay?"

Her mother looked stunned and just stared at her for a moment, until she broke down in tears. Real tears. Kat put her arms around her but said nothing.

"Satan knew the risk Kat. He couldn't stand the thought of you getting left behind after all you have done for others. It was a sacrifice he was willing to make," Amon said.

"Who is going to rule Hell?" Lyla asked.

"Satan was never an absolute ruler. Nor did he want to be. He has a board of decision makers that will keep things according to the rules as they were laid out. Hell won't change. It will continue to be the same fair, albeit imperfect, place as it was."

"All those deaths and killings in Heaven. I can't help but feel like this is all my fault, what a fucking mess," Kat was crying again. Lyla put a plump arm around her shoulders, in the exact way that Kat had done when she had dragged her to Hell.

"Those weren't real souls Kat. They were God's army, beings He created to do His dirt. The coward was never going to fight. It's all going to be okay Kat."

Kat didn't think so. Kat thought that if only she had just resolved herself to her fate in Heaven, and didn't have to be such an asshole, Satan would still be in Hell where he belonged. She looked to her mother and father again, her cats were still firmly attached to her legs. Lucifer was shaking in his armor, his fierceness gone. She hated herself for the sacrifice that Satan had made for her. His existence in Heaven would almost certainly be orgy-less. But she had people to care for here in Hell. She was afraid it might be a hard adjustment for her mother and father.

They had both entered Hell in their twenty-something bodies. Complete with scars and flaws. She put a hand to her own face, and felt it was intact. The damage that God had done to her Heaven body had been healed. The excruciating pain she had felt was gone.

"I guess I should help you get settled," Kat said to her parents. They just nodded. "Okay guys, you'll need to get off my legs. I'm not going anywhere." Buster hopped off her leg as if he hadn't been clinging on for dear life. Kat saw a few other people who had gotten through wandering around the black sand. Lyla was beginning to round them up and show them where to go. Most of them looked dazed, but more curious than scared.

"Do you promise?" Lucifer whined.

"I promise little dude," Kat plucked Lucifer off her shin and tried to nuzzle him under her chin but was thwarted by his helmet. "Maybe lose the horn though?" He shook his head, and it fell to the ground. He hopped down, seemingly reassured.

Amon took her hand, "Let's head back to Satan's place. We can get some food and rest. Jess and Alice are there and can't wait to see you. They wanted to come to, but Satan insisted they stay. He put them up in his place as his guests of honor."

Kat nodded and they began to walk in the direction of Satan's mansion which wasn't far. She really hoped that the minions had found another place to play their games. She wasn't even close to explaining all that to her mother. She figured she would ease her into the whole torture thing gradually. Maybe start with the pointy booted ass kicking and work her way from there. She didn't even want to think about how to explain the orgies.

They only made it a few steps before thunder crashed behind them. They all turned to see the sky open up one more time to drop a glowing helmetless angel into the Lake of Fire.

23

Kat turned and ran for the shore, "Satan!"

Amon followed her and clutched the back of her robe and stopped her just short of the edge before she could be burned by the lake. A small black column of smoke trickled up from where she had seen Satan drop into the liquid fire. She tried to see if there was any movement in the lake, but there was nothing. Amon let go of her robe and put an arm around her shoulder.

"It's okay babe. He'll surface. It's not like he can drown."

A ripple appeared, followed by several more, and a skeletal arm broke the surface, followed by a skull. The fleshless body began to swim toward the beach.

"I'm going to get these guys back to the mansion," Lyla said to Kat, apparently reading her thoughts. The last thing she needed was her parents meeting Satan in the flesh, except without any flesh. On a good day, he was already a little hard to look at.

While Lyla and Amon escorted her parents to Satan's mansion, Kat waited at the edge of the lake digging her toes into the soft black sand to keep from stepping into the fire.

There was a moment when she saw Satan struggling that she considered jumping in to save him. But if Satan without skin would be hard for her parents to deal with, they would really lose their shit if they had to see her that way. She was already feeling a little like a jerk leaving them in the hands of Lyla and Amon. Satan needed her. After what felt like, but objectively couldn't have been an eternity, the skeletal remains of the Prince of Darkness pulled himself up on the beach. As he emerged from the lake, he rolled over onto his back. Kat dropped to her knees and took his bloody skull into her lap.

Only small bits of flesh clung to his bones. His eyeballs rolled in their sockets to look at her. The jaw opened and closed, exposing a gaping tongueless maw. Despite having no eyelids, Satan's pain and her own concerned expression reflected in his gaze as he stared up at her.

"Oh God," Kat said as she began to weep. Satan rolled his eyes as she caught her Hell faux pax. "I mean…Oh Lemmy." She smiled in spite of herself. "Fuck, I'm so sorry……. I don't know what to do."

Satan lifted a hand and waved what was left of his once magnificent fingers. Two minions appeared with a rickshaw. Kat tried to help her friend stand, but he was too weak. She found that without any flesh, she could pick him up easily. Kat set him down carefully on the velvet lined seat and covered him with the blanket she found there. He was shivering.

"Must be a cold day in Hell," she said with a hopeful half smile.

Satan kept shivering so she couldn't tell if he appreciated the joke. He had no lips to smile with. She held him close as the minions took them to his home. They moved slowly, trying to avoid any rocks or bumps that might cause their patient any more pain.

The torture minions were not out in front of the large mansion as they pulled up. Kat took just a small amount of comfort in the fact that her parents hadn't witnessed the more unpleasant side of Hell just yet. The two minions that had been pulling the rickshaw motioned for her to step aside, as a third emerged from the front doors with a stretcher. Kat watched and then followed behind as they carefully carried him inside.

As the doors closed behind them, the three minions took Satan upstairs. The mansion was warmer than she had expected, but she figured that they had turned up the heat for the now skinless lord of the mansion. The robe she had been wearing in Heaven clung to her. She couldn't wait to put on her threadbare jeans and one of Amon's band shirts. But she would need a shower first. She still wore the glitter, or perhaps simply heavenly bird shit, and the sticky golden blood from the slaughtered angels from Heaven. She found the sparkles from Heaven to be far more offensive than any rookie stripper coated in contagious Victoria Secret body glitter had ever been. But she needed to attend to her friends and family first. She had put them all through hell. Or Heaven as seemed to be the case. The robe was becoming moist with the warmth of the room. She would check on Satan after his minions had a chance to render first aid. Although, Kat wasn't exactly sure what that was when all of your flesh had burned away.

Kat walked barefoot between the large spiral staircases and toward the sitting room. She wasn't as familiar with this part of the mansion. She had so far only been to Satan's bedroom and orgy chamber. The décor was much the same though she noticed, with one noticeable exception. Amid the deep reds, purples, and black color scheme colorful paintings were now mounted on the walls every few feet. She turned to admire a painting of a cat in a space helmet that hung on one dark red wall and recognized it from the book of manners that had graced her bedroom in Heaven. The painting contradicted the dark gothic theme of the hallway in a way that reflected Satan's goodwill and mild temperament. A pleasant mix of darkness and benevolence. Jess apparently wasted no time in making her mark in Hell. Kat couldn't restrain her joy and began to giggle. As she did, she felt her nipples brush the inside of her robe, and her smile grew wider. She was still covered in Heaven's gooey atrocities, but the insults that Heaven had inflicted on her body had been reversed.

She found who she was looking for in a small sitting room just off the side of the kitchen. More Jess art, but also some she didn't recognize adorned the walls in this room too. Amon was carefully examining one of the pieces with an odd look on his face. Her parents were sitting on a sofa opposite Jess, Alice, Lyla and a tall guy Kat didn't know. Echo snuggled up against Jess on the sofa. Kat noticed that Alice and Jess didn't look all that different from as they had in Heaven.

Jess stood up and embraced her in a bear hug, "Oh Lemmy! I'm so glad you made it!"

Kat planted a kiss on her cheek before letting her go, "The book was about the best thing in Heaven." *Aside from the donuts,* she thought.

The stranger from the sofa stood up, and held his hand out in greeting, "Hi, I'm Paul. Jess' boyfriend. Kat was just a bit disappointed, as Paul was really cute. His light-colored hair was gelled up in a point at the top of his head, and he had a beard which Kat considered optimum pussy tickling length.

"Wow, you move pretty fast," Kat said to Jess.

"Well, not really. Paul was my high school sweetheart. We were going to be married. But He died in a car accident, too soon. When I didn't find him in Heaven, I thought I'd never see him again. But now, he's my forever person."

Paul locked Jess in a long-wet kiss. Kat wasn't much for romance, but they were cute enough to make her swoon. Echo hopped down from the sofa to wind herself around the lovers' legs.

"I hope the trip wasn't too rough?" Kat said to Alice, as she walked to where Amon was frowning at another painting.

"It was way worth it. Man, it's really hard to see how bad Heaven sucks until you get to Hell."

Kat put her arms around Amon, who turned away from the painting, to hug her back before sticking his tongue in her mouth, which she accepted enthusiastically.

When she finally pulled away, he said, "Satan has done some redecorating." His frown had returned.

"Jess is an artist, a really good one," Kat replied unable to hide the defensiveness in her voice, or the frown on her own face.

"It's not art unless somebody hates it," Jess said with a staggeringly sweet smile.

Amon shrugged, "Well, I guess it's art then." Kat elbowed him hard in the ribs.

Kat left Amon to frown some more at the paintings and sat next to her parents on the sofa. A small coffee table sat in between the two couches. On it was a bottle of wine, and a plate of fruit, cheeses, and other snacks. Plus, a large pitcher of water. Kat poured herself a large glass and guzzled it, grateful to be actually thirsty again. She smiled and nodded at Lyla, who returned the gesture.

"You guys alright?"

"We're okay. Had a lovely talk with your friends here," her father said. But Kat wasn't really all that worried about him. Beelzebub, who was curled up at his feet seemed to have adjusted okay as well. At least from what Kat could tell from his dog snores. Kat was much more concerned about her mom.

"That's good, they're pretty good people," she looked at her mother tentatively, unable to read her face.

"It's not Heaven Kathryn, but maybe that's okay," her mother said. Kat wasn't sure what her mother was thinking. But she didn't want to press the issue. She looked stunned, and Kat worried that she might be traumatized. She hoped there were some good shrinks that had made it to Hell.

"Well, fill me the fuck in. What happened while I was playing pseudo-Jesus?"

Jess and Alice started to talk at the same time, but Jess' voice won, and Alice quieted to let her speak, "Accckkkk! So many things. First, we got like a fuck ton of people here. The donuts and the bird shit worked wonders. Man, so many people were miserable up there. There was a bit of a mess at registration, but Satan deputized Alice, Lyla, and I to help get them settled since we had been to Heaven already. It was actually kind of fun. Seeing the relief on their faces to be reunited with their felines and loved ones. It was really amazing."

"I introduced them to the orgies," Lyla volunteered. Kat cringed and tried to avoid looking in the direction of her parents. "I think Satan is planning a special one for those from Heaven in your honor." Kat tried to melt into the sofa she was sitting on as she felt her cheeks turn red. "Uh…some sort of big ass party anyway."

Kat's mother and father stood up together, "I think we are going to going to go to our room now. Lyla said we can stay here for a little while before we find our permanent home. You kids have fun." He smiled, aware that he and her mother looked to be the same age as the rest of the room. The afterlife was funny that way. It occurred to her that she hadn't seen any children or babies in either Heaven or Hell. But she thought that could only be a really good thing. She hoped God wasn't hiding a bunch of kids somewhere in Heaven, but even now she couldn't imagine Him being that big of an asshole.

After her parents left the room, with Beelzebub in tow, Lyla looked at her and said, "Oooo, sorry."

"Yeah, there's probably going to be an awkward conversation or two. Although, I'm still holding on to the hope that I can avoid the subject… Like… forever."

Amon joined her on the couch and snuggled up next to her. She snuggled back. Suddenly, very aware of her restored anatomy. She began to squirm a little in her seat. But she would have to wait a little longer for that kind of snuggling. Well not snuggling per se, more like raunchy demon sex.

"So, what's next for you guys?"

"Paul and I have our own place. I have a studio. My art supplies aren't quite what they were in Heaven, but they'll do."

"Yeah, mediocrity is the name of the game here," Kat shrugged.

"It's actually kind of awesome!" Jess replied. "Creativity can't thrive amid endless perfection." Kat really wished she had met Jess sooner, as she was a rich source of profound insights at just the right moments.

"Satan made me the ambassador of orgies while you were gone. I think I've found my calling." Lyla said, and Kat couldn't agree more.

"What about you?" Kat said to Alice, who had been waiting patiently to talk. Kat had been wondering how she would adjust, maybe not to Hell, but to Satan himself. She looked a little freaked out when she met him at the portal.

"Satan asked if I wanted a permanent room here. Honestly, I wasn't sure," she looked down into her lap.

"His looks are a little rough," Kat said what Alice apparently could not, or didn't want to.

"Yeah, I didn't want to be rude. It's not like I'm any kind of a supermodel myself. But once he flashed those head dicks, it was kind of hard not to like him."

"Right?" Kat laughed; she was hoping he would pull that trick.

"Any who, he kind of grew on me, and I agreed."

"Are you guys a thing?" Kat found herself swooning again.

"I mean, I don't know. But it's been fun. And I have a permanent job as a Heaven refugee coordinator, which I really like. It's really crazy how sweet that guy is. So, it will go where it goes." She smiled, blushed, and checked out her own lap again. "At least when he is healed."

"That is fucking awesome," and for the first time since going back to Heaven, Kat didn't feel like an asshole. She seemed to have really done some good.

"You ready to go home? Your cats are waiting for you," Amon said.

"I am so fucking ready," Kat said squirming in her seat again. "But I can't leave without checking on Satan. I'm fucking starving too."

"Got it. I'll get you some dinner while you see him, then we'll go home and…snuggle," he said with a devious wink.

24

Kat wasn't sure what she would find as she made her way up the carpeted stairs leading to Satan's bed chambers. He had looked pretty rough. More than normal. But in comparison to his Heaven form, it was probably the scariest thing she had seen since she had died. But love is funny like that. He was hard to look at, but only until you learned his true nature. Personality really does go a long way. She knew that he was self-conscious about how he looked to new people, or probably anyone at all. Alice's first reaction had disconcerted him enough to attempt to cover his horns and put on make-up. God's pettiness and cruelty was demonstrated in the way he looked in Heaven versus Hell. The brief glimpse she got of him in his angel form was all she needed to see how much God relied on vanity as a means of punishment and control. It was why she had learned to appreciate her blemishes and scars. She had spent her last years on earth making money on her looks, but she learned in death that they were essentially worthless. Sure, a pretty face and a great pair of tits are great to look at, but some of the most beautiful beings she had ever met, turned out to the ugliest and most vile.

Kat slowly pushed open the door to his room, which hadn't been closed all the way. She was prepared for the shock of Satan's condition, but she was not prepared for the shock of seeing her mother by his bedside. She was holding a cool cloth over his exposed eyeballs and whispering softly. Kat held her breath, afraid to move and catch the attention of her mom.

"Shhh…it's going to be okay now. Just rest," her mother said in the soft tone she had used with her when she had been sick as a child. Her mother looked up and saw Kat watching them. "I think I understand now, Kathryn."

Kat didn't know what to say. Which was kind of her thing in situations where she really needed to say something profound. She walked over and sat next to her mother on the bed. Satan's shallowing breathing was the only sound in the room.

"Amon explained that he will heal, but it will take time. I know now who the real monsters are. And it's not this beautiful angel. I think I've always known. I let my fear of the unknown override my senses. I should've never put blind faith in a God that refused to show Himself. A God that refused to hold Himself to the same standards He required of His believers. A God that required devotion and loyalty over kindness to our fellow humans. The lie of Heaven and Hell was only leverage for a narcissistic deity. I was wrong Kathryn." Her mother took her hand off the cloth covering Satan's eyes and put her arms around her only daughter. "I still wish you would have chosen another job rather than a waitress at a bar though."

Uh…sure…waitress, Kat almost said, but caught herself just in time. She wanted to push back against the dig on her earth life, but her mother had come much farther than she had expected already. And her mother had had enough truth for the moment. And maybe the rest of eternity. There was no reason to know everything.

"It's not that bad here mom. I swear."

"I know this is Hell honey, but don't swear."

Their embrace broke as they both started giggling.

"Some things kind of suck sometimes, but it's all honest. There's no weird filter or clandestine agenda. Kindness rules here. And you should see the flowers after it rains."

A woman in a nurse outfit entered the room. She didn't look like any nurse that Kat had ever seen in a hospital, but like a nurse you might see in a porn movie. Her mother frowned but to Kat's surprise, kept her lips pursed in a likely effort to keep her mouth shut. She was suddenly grateful that her mother wasn't wearing pearls, or she most certainly would have been clutching them.

The nurse was holding a clipboard and an obviously fake stethoscope. Kat and her mother stood up from the bed to let the medical professional have her space. The nurse pulled back the cloth and wrote something down on her clip board. She then opened her top to expose her breasts. Satan moved a little under the sheet and then a small, tented protrusion appeared at his blanket covered hips. Kat's mother drew in a sharp breath and grasped her neck despite being pearl-less, as she looked away.

"Take two of these, and call me in the morning," she said breathlessly before putting her giant boobs back into her costume. The nurse then turned to Kat and said in an entirely different tone, "He's going to be okay. His skin is already beginning to come back. It's going to take much less time than if he had been a human soul." She spoke directly to Kat's mother, "Louise, your cool cloth has sped the healing process considerably. Here in Hell, the most effective medicine besides laughter is compassion. You've done a great good here for a great being."

Kat's mother smiled, albeit a bit sheepishly, "That's good to know. Kathryn, can you take over for me for a little while? I'm going to go and be with your father."

"Of course, mom. I'll come get you tomorrow and if you want, we can visit the registration office and find you a permanent home."

Her mother nodded and left the room. The nurse followed behind, but not too close, which was just fine with Kat. She sat down on the bed next to Satan. Already, she could see a thin skin beginning to grow back.

"I guess I should say thank you. I'm grateful but so sorry you are going through this," Kat said in a soft voice.

"I love you, Kat," Satan croaked, and Kat almost fell off the bed.

"Holy shit! Your tongue is back," she said astonished.

"Well, mostly. I will still need some time before it's ready for the important work."

Kat removed the cloth from his eyes and saw that his lids were mostly restored. His lips still needed some work, but she was amazed at the speed of the growth. He was trying to wink and failing miserably. His smirk was a little more successful. The only thing she found odd was that there were no horns at the top of his head. She figured those must be coming later.

"Wow, you're coming back really fast."

"My nurse was correct. Love and compassion speeds healing, especially in Hell. Your mother is quite something."

Kat cringed a little, she hadn't felt that kind of love and compassion from her mother in a long time. "She's definitely something. She was very Catholic you know."

"I do know. She told me all about it. I wasn't able to respond, but I don't think I needed to," his voice was still rough and some of his words were hard to make out, but she could almost hear his facial structures healing. Each time she blinked or closed her eyes, when she opened them again, he had healed a little more. His skin appeared to thicken as it healed, but it was the unusually pale colored skin of an angel.

"It can be hard for lifetime non-believers to understand, but the myths of religion are essential for some people Kat. Belief in things that don't always make logical sense is part of being human. Superstition and magical thinking are mechanisms that allow for some to deal with life itself. Some wield those beliefs as a weapon to divide and hurt others. Or sometimes just for their own personal or political gain. But not all of them. Some are only following what they were told or looking for guidance in a world that no one, whether a God or a man completely understands. Don't ever believe anyone who tells you they know the absolute truth about life and death and what may come after. No one does and probably never will, but everyone human or not still craves those answers. Anyone who tells you they have them is only exploiting the desire to know for sure. Your mother is a good person. She always has been, and she only wanted the best for you, even if she never quite understood you."

A river of tears that would have never fallen in Heaven ran down her face and landed on the blanket that covered the Prince of Darkness. The being she had been taught was pure evil, was really just a being trying to figure everything out himself. Kat lifted up part of her robe to dry her face, when she dropped it and opened her eyes, she saw that Satan had progressed even farther in his healing. Blonde hair covered his skull, and creamy white skin covered the muscle on his bones. Golden eyelashes had sprouted from his eyelids, while rose covered lips covered his teeth. He was healing into his angelic form. He lifted his hand and wiped a tear from her cheek. She noticed with only slight disappointment that his fingers were more delicate and slender than they had been before. He smiled at her.

"Thank you," was all she could think of to say.

Satan rose up to a sitting position to hug her, "It's all going to be okay. Go be with your demon and your fucking cats. They're waiting for you. You've done well, Kat."

Kat squeezed him tighter and felt something tickle her face. As she pulled away, she saw the golden curls of his hair had reached his shoulders. His broad muscled shoulders. She thought about hanging out just a bit longer, but he was right, her demon and cats were waiting for her. And as hot as angelic Satan was, she missed her man. She kissed him on his perfect cheek, and he watched her leave his room. Two more nurses, or maybe just previously living porn stars in nurse outfits stood just outside his door, along with a minion carrying a silver platter, the contents of which smelled amazing. Kat nodded and the three entered Satan's room.

As Kat made her way down the stairs, a minion met her at the bottom wearing a butler's collar and tie and nothing else. They took her arm and led her to the large dining room. An enormous feast was waiting. Her mouth watered and she realized that she was ravenous. Amon stood at the head of the table and stood when she entered the room.

"I had the chefs whip up a little something," Amon said.

Alice, Lyla, Paul, and Jess all stood up to greet her as the butler minion pulled out her chair. The table was laden with everything she could have possibly imagined. Roast chicken and beef and pork, pasta, fresh fruit and steamed and sauteed vegetables graced the table. And at the center was a large platter of donuts. Kat sat down and had no clue where to begin. So, she just took some of everything and began to eat.

The butler minion poured her a glass of wine before sitting down himself, along with all the other mansion minions. Satan's minions all had jobs, but she had never seen them treated as anything other than equal beings. They smiled and ate with polite gusto. They didn't speak but smiled happily between bites.

Kat joked and laughed with her friends as they ate. Her food was slightly overcooked, under-seasoned, too salty, or too bland, too chunky, or too smooth, but it was all the best food she had ever eaten. She couldn't remember ever being so grateful or happy in all of her life or death.

When she felt like she had eaten until she was about to burst, she tossed her napkin on her plate and sat back in her chair. She was very aware that she was in dire need of a shower and fresh clothes. They only reason she was still wearing her glitter defiled robe was in consideration of her parents.

"You ready?" Amon said.

"Holy fuckballs, yes. Take me to bed or lose me forever," she said.

Kat said goodbye to her friends, and she walked with Amon to the front doors, where they found a minion waiting to give them a lift back to her house. The night sky was a beautiful hellscape. The stars or whatever they were, lit up the sky. The moist night air carried the light scent of copper, and she thought a storm might be on the way. Her suspicions were proven correct as they pulled up to her door. A small drop of blood landed on her forehead as she stepped down from the rickshaw. They waved to the minion as they scurried off into the night.

Lucifer jumped into her arms as she opened the doors, while Buster scowled from the sofa. The acrid scent of cat shit haunted the air.

"Kat, Kat… I missed you so much," her furry heaven turned hellcat said. He began to furiously lick her face.

"Ok dude. That's enough. I need to take a shower," she said.

"You really do though," he said. "Look at this first though." He turned to her and lifted his tail. "It's lovely little buddy," she said to him.

Kat patted Buster on the head and scratched under his chin and he began to purr in spite of himself. Before they had left Satan's mansion, Amon packed up some of the cat-friendly leftovers. He took those into the kitchen and began to divide them among the two dishes that sat on opposite sides of the little table.

"Go get cleaned up, I'll take care of the cat box," Amon said with a grimace. Kat wasn't sure what was grosser, her or the cat box.

As the warm water rinsed the horrors of Heaven off of her body, Kat heard the bloody rain began to patter on the roof. Thunder rolled gently outside as she toweled off. She wrapped her hair with it when she was done and plucked the offensive robe off the floor as she left the bathroom. Lucifer was standing outside the door staring at her. He didn't say anything but followed her to the living room where Amon snatched the robe out of her hands with a sneer.

"I'm going to put this with the cat shit," he said.

Lucifer followed her into her bedroom and hopped up on the bed. Still quietly staring at her as if she was the most magnificent thing he had ever seen. Given that he had been created specifically for her, she guessed she probably was. His ears flattened as Amon entered the room, stripped, and joined them on the bed. Kat picked up the furry little guy and nuzzled him under her chin before setting him just outside the door.

"It's snuggle time little dude. I love you. I'll see you in the morning."

Lucifer pouted, turned and lifted his tail as she shut the door to her room.

25

Kat awoke to the sound of furious scratching on her bedroom door. Amon rolled out of bed to open it. Lucifer charged in and jumped on top of her, he had a dark red envelope in his mouth. He dropped it on her face.

"I'll go start the coffee," Amon said, and Kat was impressed that he didn't sound annoyed as he looked. His hair stood up in unkempt spikes and his eyes didn't look like they wanted to open all the way.

"This came this morning. Open it," her talking cat said.

She had to remove him from her chest to sit up. She opened the envelope and pulled out what looked like a formal invitation. It read: *You are cordially invited to the celebration of Kat's triumphant return. Please come in your best attire. There will be food and drink and entertainment. An after-party orgy will be available to all who wish to participate. Please remember to wash your genitals and bring your own towel. It starts tonight at 7pm.*

"How nice to be formally invited to my own party," Kat giggled as Amon returned with two steaming mugs of coffee. Buster trotted in behind him and hopped up on the bed.

Kat scratched Buster between the ears with one hand while taking the mug of coffee that Amon was holding out to her with the other.

"What did it say?" Amon asked as he slid under the covers displacing the cats and earning himself duel dirty looks.

"It's my welcome back party and orgy," she said hoping that her parents invite didn't include the orgy part. The hedonistic sex parties were her favorite part of Hell, but she hadn't considered how awkward they would be now that her parents were in Hell too. She really hoped that Satan had planned a contingency for that. "Tonight at 7."

"That sounds awesome," Amon turned and kissed her on the cheek. The light from the window cast an orange glow on his face. The passing rainstorm had left the glass smeared in blood. "I'll take care of the windows. Why don't you figure out what you're going to wear while I do that?"

"Sounds like a plan. I would like to check on my mom and dad, and Satan. But I'm guessing he's good to go if he planned the party tonight."

A light knock sounded on the door, and Kat cocked her head to the sound. She wasn't expecting anyone, which meant it was probably Lyla. She got up and threw on a worn bath robe. Nothing like the foul thing she had been wearing the night before. A once really fluffy terry cloth bath robe that had seen better days but had enough life in it to still be cozy.

She pulled open the door and said, "Morning Ly...Oh hi," she said to her parents, clinching her robe tighter.

Her mother looked at her tangled hair and frowned, "Good morning, Kathryn. We were on our way to our new home and thought we would stop by."

"Come in. Amon made some coffee, and I think we might have some donuts," Kat said as she stepped aside to allow them to enter with Beelzebub following behind.

Kat showed them to her small kitchen table which conveniently had four chairs. Amon brought them coffee and a plate of golden donuts, then sat down to join them.

Kat's father sipped his coffee with a grimace, "Thanks. It's great."

"You don't have to lie to kick it, Dave. Have a bit more sugar. After the first few sips, it's not bad." Kat's dad smiled and dumped a hefty tablespoon of sugar from the chipped sugar bowl that sat on the table into his coffee.

"Yup, that's better. We've been given a little place just down the road," her father said.

"They said there is a nice spot in the backyard for a garden," her mother said. She had added an obscene amount of sugar to her coffee and was reaching for a donut. "I think you might be right about the flowers here Kathryn. They are quite pretty. I think I want to grow some veggies too," she said as she eyed her donut before taking a bite.

"You'll love it," she told her mom.

"We're looking forward to the party tonight," her father said. "There's an after party that promises a fireside reading of Moby Dick. Your mother and I are quite excited about it," he took another sip of his coffee, but this time, without the look of disgust. "We're very proud of you."

Kat let out the breath she had been holding. Satan might have been a shitty planner, but he really came through when he needed to. "That's great!"

"I think we have another after party to attend, but you guys will have fun," Amon said, Kat frowned at him.

They sat and talked for a little while. Amon offered to help build the garden, but her parents said they were looking forward to building it themselves. Kat was still getting used to seeing them in their younger forms, but she figured that would fade soon enough. They got up and said their goodbyes again. Beelzebub had been chilling in the living room seemingly unperturbed by the two cats who were obviously trying to stare him to death.

Amon did the chores as promised as Kat looked for something to wear. She found a dark red off the shoulder dress and a pair of black pumps that had only a small scuff on the side. She set the dress and shoes aside.

"I'm going to head back to my place and get ready. I'll be back this evening to pick you up," Amon said when he had finished his work. "Oh…and I'm taking Lucifer with me. He wants to go tonight also, and I promised him I would help him find something to wear."

"Okay, see you," Kat kissed him on the cheek and watched as he and Lucifer left.

Kat didn't think it was weird that Lucifer would want to go to the party, she did think it odd that he wanted to get ready with Amon. But the damned cat had been weird from the moment they met, so she put the thought out of her head quickly. Buster looked content to stay home. It wasn't hard to tell which had been a real cat.

As the time grew closer, Kat sat on the sofa with Buster in her lap. She would have cat hair on her dress but didn't care. Her dress didn't have a rip, stain or worn spot on it. It looked brand new in fact, so she thought a bit of cat hair was just the thing for a ball in Hell. She was listening for the sound of Amon's motorcycle, so the knock at the door startled her. She brushed Buster off her lap and got up to meet Amon.

"Why didn't…" she had been trying to ask why he didn't just come in, but it was Lyla that stood there and not her demon. "Hey. Oh wow, you look stunning," Kat said.

Lyla wore a dark purple gown with a plunging neckline. It hugged every curve.

"You look pretty good yourself. You ready?" Lyla said, and Kat could see a black gothic carriage behind her. Inside sat Amon with Lucifer on his lap and a couple of towels on the seat beside him. Lucifer had on a small red bowtie. Two thick, black-horned demon horses stood attached. They snorted impatiently and blew red puffs of smoke out of their nostrils.

"I am so ready," Kat said, but Lyla stopped her before she could come out of the door.

"Did you remember a hair tie?"

Kat smacked a palm to her forehead, "Nope. Hang on." She darted back inside and slipped a black scrunchy around her wrist. "Ha! I got it." So far, she had always been the chick who forgot to bring a hair tie to the orgy.

She followed Lyla to the carriage and hopped in. The two horses were off in a flash. They moved so fast and so light that she wondered if they were flying instead of running. The scenery flashed past her in what seemed like an instant, and then they were at Satan's mansion. A very long but orderly line of Hell's inhabitants streamed in through double doors. Kat knew there was no way that everyone in Hell had come, but it certainly looked like it.

Once inside, they were led to an enormous ballroom. The room was so large, she couldn't even see the edges of the room. It looked as if it went on forever. Large screens hung from the ceiling. Amon and Lyla were shown to their table close to the stage. And soon she understood the screens. There was simply no logistical way that everyone would be able to see the stage without them. She was seated at the table with Alice and Paul and Jess.

The lights went dim, and Satan stepped on stage. His blond curly hair framed his face and touched his shoulder. Large gold and white feathered wings poked through the back of his black velour jogging suit. When she had first met him, the very sight of him scared her so badly she had thought she would faint. She had grown used to the sight of him, she wasn't sure if she would ever get used to seeing him as he looked in Heaven. The crowd hushed as he began to speak.

"We are here tonight to honor Kat, but also the brave souls who sought kindness and truth over the pettiness and cruelties of Heaven and sacrificed its perfection. We are happy to have all who have made it here and I will try my best to make eternity as pleasant as possible. I won't be long up here, as we have one hell of a show for you tonight!" He paused for a reaction to his pun with a huge corny grin on his face, which

Kat noticed had taken on a funny shade of pink. "First up is Alice. Come up here."

Alice stood up blushing and stepped up to the stage. In Hell, she wore large glasses which reflected the stage lights. She smiled and bowed as Satan greeted her.

"I present to you the gratitude of Hell for your brave efforts in helping so many people get to Hell." Satan handed her a bronze statue of herself. The statue version of her looked like a mega store greeter. Complete with cheesy vest. He grabbed and kissed her before sending her on her way. One of Satan's angelic wings fell to the stage, but the crowd didn't seem to notice.

Next came Lyla, who received a large golden dildo as she was congratulated for her new role as the Orgy Ambassador to Hell. As she bowed, her dress split up the back with a loud rip. She began to laugh as Satan gave it a slight tug, and the whole thing came apart. Lyla bowed again holding the giant gold dick, but this time wearing only a strapless purple teddy and stockings. Satan lost the other wing, and Kat saw two bumps rise out of his blond hair which had begun to fall to the floor in golden tufts.

Then Jess, whose award came in the form of a silver paint palette came after. She had been crowned Satan's personal artist and interior decorator. As she stepped down, a funny mummering came over the crowd as they finally noticed that something was wrong.

Satan's face had widened at the jaw, his wings lay on the stage and the bumps on his head had grown and his skin went from baby pink to dark red. He was becoming the monster he had been.

"Don't be alarmed my friends!" He boomed from the stage and all of the screens. "I am only coming back into my Hell form." By the time he finished his sentence, he was back to the way she had met him. "But let us not be distracted by such a silly little thing from the reason we are here!" He shook his head, and smoke began to curl up from his horns.

The crowd cheered. "Kat! Get your ass up here!" Kat did as she was told. "We have a special honor for you this evening. But you probably guessed that already." Kat nodded her head. "Because the honor of martyr was so rudely stolen from you," Satan winked. "We have arranged to right that wrong."

Kat was a little confused and wondered if Satan was going to nail her to a cross. Lucifer, who had snuck on stage when she wasn't looking, appeared on stage and stood looking up at Satan with a toothy cat grin. Satan picked him up in his arms, making him look tiny.

"Your selfless act that saved so many from the lies and misery of Heaven, we all thought that you should at least have the same honor as the son of God has enjoyed." Satan began to glow red. "Thanks to you, I will reign in Hell and all who inhabit it. You, Kat, have been chosen to honor me in the way the Jesus was chosen to honor God."

Kat waited for the cross to appear behind him and was almost sure that she had grossly misjudged not only Satan, but the whole situation. Had she only been a pawn in this holy warfare? Her Sunday school teachings came roaring back to her. The father of lies, the Prince of Darkness, the antichrist, all of a sudden fear gripped her and she was sure that she had royally fucked up.

Satan abruptly lifted little Lucifer over his head and now terrifying horns, the poor little thing looked helpless in his grip. He turned the cat around and the crowd gasped.

Kat closed her eyes and waited for what was going to come next, sure that whatever it was, it was probably going to hurt. But when she heard the Oooooo's and Aaaaaaahh's from the crowd, she opened them again.

She was greeted by the sight of Lucifer's butt. Still confused, but way less terrified. But as she looked a pattern began to appear. It looked like a face. Then it looked like her face. Her face created in fur and sphincter. Her face depicted perfectly in Lucifer's cat ass.

26

After the main festivities and entertainment had ended and after Kat explained to her parents that the towels and hair tie were for the pool and spa after party they were attending, she found herself once again in Satan's orgy chamber. There had been several rooms opened up to allow for the sheer number of people who had wanted to join. Each room catered to different tastes and fetishes.

Kat expected Alice to be there, and she was making the most out of the experience, with Satan as her guide. She hadn't expected to see Paul and Jess there, but it turned out that her new friends were a bit more freaky than she might have guessed. She found herself at one point making out with Jess and decided that this friendship might just take an unexpected, but very welcome turn.

By the time that the sun began to crawl up over the horizon, the orgy had dispersed. Kat laid in Amon's arms as Satan passed around the goat horn pipe. Jess, Paul, and Alice all laid with them on the giant shag rug and plush pillows. They avoided talk of God and Heaven and the strange trip they had all taken. Instead, the conversation turned to talk of

Lyla's wedding and the inevitable orgy that would happen, and their own plans for an eternity in Hell. As bowl after bowl turned to ash, they each fell into an exhausted, but contented slumber.

Outside, in a portion of Hell that had yet to be occupied, a tiny white cloud floated in the sky. A pale golden light flashed, and a light drizzle of glitter began to fall.

The End

About the Author

Erin Louis is a former adult entertainer with three non-fiction books about her life as a stripper as well as several short fiction stories.

She has a lifelong love of horror and dark humor.

Please check out her website at https://www.erinlouis.com/

OTHER HELLBOUND BOOKS

www.hellboundbooks.com

South of Heaven

Kat, a lapsed Catholic and promiscuous stripper, never thought she would get into Heaven.

Even as she stands there at the Pearly Gates, she naturally expects to be sent directly to Hell. She picks a fight with St. Peter just for fun, but rules are rules, and Kat makes it into Heaven on a minor technicality.

Once there, Kat discovers, much to her dismay, the angels are jerks, the only music is God-awful Christian rock, and her brand-new halo comes with some most troubling conditions.

As if things weren't dismaying enough, Kay reunites with her father, who found eternal peace in a bottomless bottle of scotch, and her pot-smoking aunt, whose demon dealer resides in Hell. When she tracks down the demon, he tells Kat about his home in the desolate, fiery pit - where it rains blood but possesses all the earthly pleasures she misses so much in her disappointing afterlife.

Heaven isn't the paradise Kat was promised in Sunday school, and she wants out.

But will they let her go?

Stripper Noir

"I'm pretty much out of my "detective phase" now that I've finished Random, but I wanted to check it out. It's a nice detective murder thing with a twist and a very nice look at Vegas and the strip club scene. It's very accurate (as far as I know) strip club description and you never see that in a book, so that was nice. And a nice view of Vegas one doesn't usually get. I really enjoyed it." - Penn Jillette

Exotic Dancers are dying at an alarming rate in Las Vegas. Former LVPD detective, Frank Michi, is roped into helping not only his former partner, but also the New Jersey mobsters who run the strip club, to unmask the psychopath who is running amok killing the dancers.

Can he figure it out in time - before more girls are brutally murdered?

Colleen

"Sexy, intriguing, terrifying - Colleen has it all! " - James H. Longmore, author of *Tenebrion.*

Lacey, a goth introvert with sketchy people skills, befriends Colleen, a dazzlingly beautiful ghost, during a solo Ouija board session. At last, her loneliness comes to an end. An eclectic pairing indeed, but they form an odd-but-satisfying and far-from-platonic friendship.
When Lacey begins work as a stripper, she and Colleen find themselves with a conspiratorial mystery to solve in the strip club.
Unfortunately, Lacey's newfound supernatural lover has a secret… or two and isn't what she seems to be at all.
Colleen is not a ghost at all, but a succubus with an unfortunate habit of killing people.
Accidentally.
It's not long before the mounting number of deaths occurring around Lacey draws the attention of a tenacious homicide detective…
Can Colleen uncover the shady happenings at the club and keep her beloved Lacey out of jail?

And Then You Die

Following a drunken, hedonistic night out in New Orleans, highly successful businesswoman and sexual deviant, Claire Jepson, accidentally soils herself in her car. The resulting excrement comes to life as a sardonic fecal spirit, and not only dishes out a gruesome death to Claire's unfaithful, gold-digging fiancé, but also thwarts a kidnap/murder plot by her employees. It then introduces Claire to a world of depraved pleasures beyond her imagination.

A year later, the errant spirit has spiraled wildly out of control - its insatiable appetite for perverted sex and human flesh and has destroyed Claire's life. Then, to her horror, Claire discovers the fecal spirit must consume her unborn child to attain immortality; she must return to the seedy underbelly of the Big Easy in a heart-pounding race against time to confront the spirit's creator - a high priest of an ancient, deadly order, who is the only one who can put a stop to the spirit's murderous intentions.

A wicked, fast-paced story laced with tongue-in-cheek, dark humor, which is at the same time incredibly erotic and stomach churning. Most definitely not one to be read whilst eating!

**A HellBound Books LLC
Publication**

www.hellboundbooks.com

www.ingramcontent.com/pod-product-compliance
Lightning Source LLC
Chambersburg PA
CBHW020802310726
48969CB00002B/662